Presented to

    for good work and
faithful attendance.
South Side Nazarene
Sunday School -
   March 8 - 1959
       H DeBard, teacher

INDIAN DRUMS AND
BROKEN ARROWS

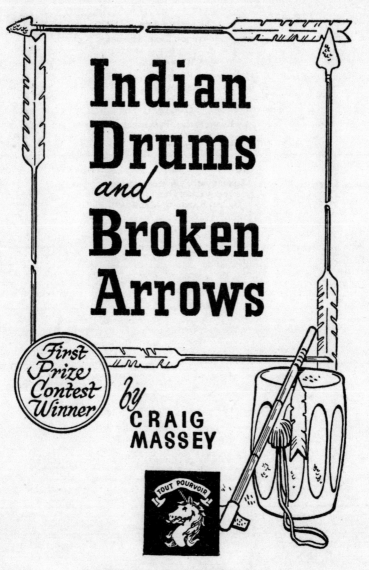

Indian Drums and Broken Arrows

First Prize Contest Winner

by CRAIG MASSEY

TOUT POURVOIR

OLIPHANTS LIMITED
LONDON :: EDINBURGH

OLIPHANTS LTD.
LONDON: 1-5 PORTPOOL LANE, HOLBORN, E.C.1.

AUSTRALIA
119 BURWOOD ROAD, BURWOOD, E.13,
MELBOURNE.

CANADA
EVANGELICAL PUBLISHERS,
241 YONGE STREET,
TORONTO.

U.S.A.
ZONDERVAN PUBLISHING HOUSE,
1415 LAKE DRIVE, S.E.
GRAND RAPIDS 6, MICHIGAN.

THIS EDITION   1958

PRINTED IN GREAT BRITAIN BY
LOWE & BRYDONE (PRINTERS) LTD., LONDON, N.W.10.

This book is lovingly
dedicated to my wife
LOUISE
and daughter
LINDA

CONTENTS

1

"Boy, Tend Them Oxen!"

A SPECKLED BREASTED song sparrow flew to an oak tree and filled the early dawn with music. As though it were a signal, other birds joined the chorus; a robin sang from a budding maple, a fiery red cardinal whistled happily from an elm and a dusky gray catbird called from a blackberry thicket. Overhead a broad winged, red-shouldered hawk circled in the first rays of the warm spring sunshine.

The smooth flowing Mohawk River was almost hidden under a misty haze off to the south. Its placid surface was suddenly broken when a glistening trout swirled upward for a low flying insect. Another trout arched into the air, snapped a moth and flashed away.

Jeff Lockwood, curled under a blanket beside the smouldering campfire, saw all these things, feeling the tingling wave of his first springtime in the wilderness flash over him. Even the hulking, snoring form of Gustave Kittle sleeping on the other side of the fire did not dim his happiness.

Jeff studied the heavy jowled face that showed from one end of the blanket. *He looks just like an old lazy snapping turtle*, Jeff thought. *A big ugly snapper, and just as ornery.*

Beyond the sleeping man stood two heavy wheeled ox-carts with bags of grain poking from under tattered canvas coverings. The four broad-chested black oxen were quietly munching the rich grass along the river bank.

Jeff stood up and folded his blanket. Then he stooped over the fire and fanned the embers into a flame, adding fuel until it danced with life. Suddenly an explosive snort came from the sleeping fat man. Jeff turned to see two pale blue eyes set deep in fleshy cheeks glaring suspiciously at him.

"You're fixin' to run off with my wagons I'll wager!" the man rasped. "From now on don't ya move from yer blanket until I give ya word."

Used to Kittle's constant scolding, Jeff remained silent, placing a pot of coffee on the fire and laying two trout in a greased spider.

While breakfast cooked Kittle fell asleep, snoring and heaving, until Jeff slid one of the fish on a square of birch bark and shook the ponderous man's shoulder, "Mr. Kittle, Mr. Kittle, wake up. Your breakfast's ready!"

The man opened his eyes and pushed a thick hand from under the blanket toward the fish. Only when he wanted to drink his coffee did he lurch to a sitting position.

After the third cup, Kittle barked at Jeff, "Get them oxen yoked. We gotta' git movin'!"

Within minutes the oxen were readied. Kittle waddled to the smaller of the oxcarts, struggled aboard and settled himself on the plank seat. His tremendous body seemed almost as wide as the wagon itself, Jeff thought.

The trail to the west was soggy with spring rains. Each time the oxen stepped their hoofs sucked mud and the wide cart wheels sank deep, oozing black slime along the rims.

An hour's slow going infuriated Kittle. With unexpected savageness he drew a thick black whip from its socket and lashed the broad backs of the struggling oxen. The wagon lurched into a fallen tree and tilted dangerously towards the river. Again the angry swishing lash curled out over the oxen and the ponderous man grunted in disgust.

Wondering at the boiling temper, Jeff steered around the log. Kittle seemed out of place in the wilderness. His great soft body did not fit into the pattern of this wild country where men were slender and hard muscled from outdoor life.

In fact, Jeff thought, *it's hard to figure just where that kind of a man does fit in, but surely not in the woods.*

Ten days earlier Jeff had been in Albany, the thriving trading center on the Hudson River, looking for a wagon train headed west along the Mohawk River. Because of the raiding Indians who were plundering the valley few men were risking the trip. It was not until he heard that Gustave Kittle wanted a driver for an oxcart, that Jeff's chance came.

"I want to take two wagon loads of grain to the farmers out there," Kittle explained when Jeff talked to him, "but I can't find a driver. If you want the job, I'll give you seventy-five cents a week and food."

Jeff leaped at the offer, not caring about the wages, but thinking only of the chance to get to Fort Stanwix where his father had gone the year before. His father had promised to return in the fall, but not a word had been heard from him since. So Jeff had decided to journey westward and trace the missing man, leaving his mother and fourteen-year-old sister, Mary, tending their bakery shop in Albany.

The trees were just turning green the day he left the bustling city limits. Mrs. Lockwood and Mary saw Jeff off, waving handkerchiefs in the distance as the wagons rolled out of sight.

Travel the first two days was speedy, but when they hit the wilderness trail it slowed down to a snail's pace. More than once the wagons bogged down in the mud.

After one particularly hard haul, Jeff said, "Mr. Kittle, it seems to me the wagons are loaded too heavy for the oxen."

Kittle exploded, "You weren't asked to tell me that. I hired you to drive and I'll do the worrying. You lash those beasts, drive them on, I say!"

Now ten days had passed. The oxen were tired but still

Kittle bullied them. At noon he drew up in a clearing beside the river. "We'll stop over here for an hour. You hustle your fish lines out and catch some dinner. I'm going to sleep."

Jeff unyoked the animals while Kittle curled up under his blanket, beginning to snore almost at once. After up-turning stones along the bank for a handful of worms, Jeff moved along the river, fishing as he went. The trout weren't feeding, but pumpkinseeds and perch were hungry and in a short time nine fish dangled from the forked branch he was using for a stringer.

It was enough for dinner, but Jeff was glad to be out of reach of his scolding employer for a little while, so he pushed his way upstream for a half mile.

Unexpectedly he broke out on the edge of a two acre clearing among the trees. A smoky, unpleasant odor reached his nostrils, making him wrinkle his face in distaste. Across the clearing he saw a charred, blackened spot. Skirting the edge of a sprouting wheat field Jeff worked his way around until he saw several half burned timbers standing like black sentinels against the blue river water.

"Indians," Jeff breathed, glancing around as though he half expected to see bronzed figures lurking in the woods.

As he drew closer he wondered what had happened to the settlers who had lived there. *Perhaps they were taken prisoners, or even killed,* he thought, remembering the hor-rifying reports of the raiding Mohawks and the torture they practiced.

He found the ashes still warm when he poked around with a stick among the scorched ruins. "That means the red-skins must have been here within the last few days. I'd better get back and tell Kittle."

Kittle was still wheezing explosively under his blanket when Jeff awakened him, "Mr. Kittle, up ahead a half mile I found a newly burned cabin. We'd better watch for Indians."

"Don't worry none. Them redskins are friends of mine," Kittle laughed.

"But the Mohawks are siding with the English against the settlers," Jeff said.

"Think nuthin' of it. I said them Mohawks are friends of mine, so don't let it bother you. Now get them fish fried up fer me."

While Jeff built the fire he began to wonder about Kittle. It seemed strange that he should be so sure the Indians were his friends — the same Indians who raided the settlements to kill and burn.

After they finished eating Kittle drew a smudged map from his pocket. Using a twig to trace the route, he grunted in satisfaction. "We'll hit the village of Oatfield this afternoon. We'll rest a day and then push on. But I'm warnin' ya fair, don't go talkin' to anybody without being asked, or I'll whip ya fer it."

As Kittle had said, they reached Oatfield in late afternoon. There were nine log cabins crowded together and beyond them stood the fort, a grim barrier of logs with the blockhouse rising above tree level.

Kittle drove up to a building quite a bit larger than the others. Over the door, framed in wooden letters, Jeff saw the words, "Stiles Warehouse and Store."

Three men, each with a musket, sat on a split log bench in front. A big, friendly shepherd dog barked a few times and sniffed curiously at the oxen. When the creaking wagons stopped, a tall, slender, white-bearded man came to the open doorway and looked out. Jeff supposed, and rightly so, that this was Mr. Stiles, the owner of the store.

One of the men on the bench pushed his hat back on his head and stared at Kittle in open dislike. "Well, if it ain't fat Gus Kittle come back again."

A short red-faced man, with fiery hair to match, looking

all the world like a red rooster, questioned, "Going west with another load of grain fer the settlers this spring, aye?"

Kittle climbed slowly from the wagon, "It's a good way to make money," he answered.

Mr. Stiles rubbed his long white beard, "I can't figure you out, Kittle. For the last three years you've managed to come through the Mohawk Valley without meeting trouble. It's uncanny. Indians have been raiding all along the river. Why, just day before yesterday a cabin was burned just east of here — family all killed. And here you are with not even a scratch to show fer it. It's mighty funny to me."

Kittle flashed angrily for a moment and then controlled himself, "I guess it's all in knowin' how to do it."

"Or knowin' them that hates the settlers. Like bein' over friendly with the British or the redskins," the rooster man snorted.

Anger again swept Kittle's face and he started to reply in a sharp voice, but Mr. Stiles interrupted. "How much are you asking for the stuff this time?"

"Three dollars a bushel, take it or leave it," Kittle snapped.

"I'll leave it," Mr. Stiles laughed. "Why, man, that's two dollars more than I get for it here at the store. Besides, it's going to be slim pickings this year. Most of the cabins have been burned along the valley."

"Them's the ones that'll have to buy my seed, them that's been burned out."

Mr. Stiles said softly, "Kittle, how you can charge them poor folks like that is beyond me. They've lost about everything, including some of their loved ones, and you try and rob them of their last few dollars."

"Have you seen Jacob Haynes?" Kittle questioned.

"Ain't seen his face since last fall, and hope I don't ever see it again. I don't like the way he runs off to Canada so often. Makes me think he's in thick with the British," the rooster man replied.

Kittle ignored him and ordered Jeff, "Drive them wagons behind the store there. Water the oxen and grease the wheels. Then rustle me up my supper. When you're ready I'll be waiting here."

Jeff took one wagon over and returned to take the other. Kittle was busy talking to the men on the bench. Mr. Stiles, his narrow shoulders hunched over a bench just inside the store, was separating beaver, mink and otter pelts.

The storekeeper glanced up and beckoned with a long gnarled finger. Jeff walked over and slipped inside the door out of sight of the arguing Kittle.

"Now, lad, what's your name?" Mr. Stiles looked at Jeff from under white shaggy eyebrows.

"Jefferson Lockwood, sir, from Albany."

"Now, what are you doing with that man Kittle? You don't look like the kind to be hiking around with his lot."

"It wouldn't be my choice, sir, but I must get westward to Fort Stanwix."

Mr. Stiles smelled one of the pelts and tossed it into a pile, "And why, now, do you have to get to the fort?"

The warm interest in the man's voice drew Jeff to a deep liking for him. "Well, sir, last year my father went west from Albany on a mission for Captain Lemming. He was supposed to return last fall but no word has come from him. We, my mother, sister and I, worked in our bakery shop, but with spring I decided to come west and find my father."

"So your father was sent by Captain Lemming. That means then, you aren't favoring the English like I suspect Kittle is?"

"No, sir, I want my country to be free and make a great nation of this territory, Mr. Stiles," Jeff said earnestly.

"Good, good!" Mr. Stiles stroked the prime fur of a

B

long martin pelt. "But this wilderness is a hard place for a boy your age. Just how old are you?"

"Sixteen, sir."

"Well, I trust you will find your father. I don't want to make you fearful, but many a man in this wilderness has felt the sharp knife of a Mohawk warrior."

"We have heard the reports back in Albany, sir. It's hearing those things that brings me out here for word of my father."

Mr. Stiles straightened up from his task and drew his hand down his beard. He seemed thoughtful, and finally peered closely at Jeff, "Lockwood — now come to think of it, I remember a man by that name who came through here last spring. A tall man, dark like yourself, with a white horse, if I recall correctly."

"That's right!" Jeff's heart leaped at the description.

"It's odd I never heard of him after that. He never came back this way, that I know."

For a few minutes neither spoke. Jeff wondered about his father. Was he still alive? Or was he a victim of the Indians who had turned the valley red and black with killings and burnings?

Mr. Stiles broke in upon his thoughts, "Say now, Jeff, don't go further with Kittle. He's no good. Stay here with me. I need help in the store. There's good money in trading for fur and you could learn trading fast."

"No, I must go west."

"But you'll likely not find him. Anyway, at least wait until you find a better man than Kittle to travel with."

"No, I can't. I promised my mother and sister to search till word turned up, and I'd never rest content unless I did."

At that moment Kittle shuffled up to the door, his face glowering with fury. "You, boy, I told you to tend them oxen! Now git!"

2

"At Least Twenty Redskins"

JEFF LOOSED and watered the oxen, greased the creaking wheels, knocked the caked mud off the spokes, and within an hour walked toward the store to report to Kittle, who still squatted on the log bench talking to the men.

A woman's voice, pleasant and friendly, hailed him from Stiles' store. "You must be Jefferson Lockwood."

"Yes, ma'am," he turned to see a plump, motherly woman coming towards him. Her hair, light as pounded wheat, was drawn back in a tight bun. Her face crinkled with a thousand lines as she smiled, "I'm Sarah Stiles. My husband has been telling me about you. We would be very pleased if you would take the evening meal with us. It's not often we have visitors from Albany, and there's lots I'd like to know. Some of my folks live back there."

"I would like to very—" but Kittle's voice broke in.

"You won't be taking supper with nobody but me. Now get back to them wagons and build a fire!"

The temptation to leave Kittle's cranky company for good flared in Jeff, but the thought of his missing father bridled his tongue. With a glance of apology toward Mrs. Stiles he obeyed.

Kittle followed, still growling, "I'm payin' you to work fer me. I won't have you goin' off whenever you take a mind to!" He paused a moment, then continued. "We'll stay here 'til tomorrow afternoon when I expect a friend of mine to show up and go with us the rest of the way."

"Who?" Jeff questioned.

"Jake Haynes."

"That's the fellow the red-haired man said was in harness with the English, isn't it?"

Kittle snorted, but didn't answer the question. Instead he ordered, "Here's a few eggs and corn meal I bought from Stiles. Rustle me up a meal."

Jake Haynes arrived about three the next day. He was a runt of a man, beady eyed, with a long nose hooked sideways, making him appear as though he were snooping around corners all the time, Jeff thought.

Haynes immediately went into conference with Kittle, talking earnestly, but so low Jeff could not hear what was being said.

When they finished, Kittle called, "Lockwood! Ready the carts, we're moving on."

The wagons rolled past the store with Kittle and Haynes leading the way. Jeff saw Mr. and Mrs. Stiles emerge from the building and wave to him. He drew the yoke to a halt to say goodbye.

Mr. Stiles slipped him a package, "Here, Jeff, this is for you. Don't let the others know about it."

Kittle stormed, "You, Lockwood, git a move on!"

"If you ever want a job out here, don't forget what I told you," Mr. Stiles called as Jeff urged the oxen onward.

They pushed along the Mohawk River westward through the valley until darkness found them in a dense pine grove. After supper the two men drew aside and talked. Jeff used the opportunity to investigate the package from Mr. Stiles. It contained a pound of golden maple sugar. After the long days with little else but fish and cornbread, it was a real treat.

Finally Jeff curled in his blanket while the men still

whispered. He made believe he had fallen asleep. The men dropped some of their caution and Haynes grunted, "Yer a fool fer bringing that kid, Kittle."

A nasal laugh escaped the fat man, "I'm no fool. We'll make money on him. He's young, and as strong as one of them oxen. The English will give us plenty fer him. If they don't, we can turn him over to the Indians. Besides, he'll come in handy fer us until we get rid of the load."

So that was Kittle's plan! *Well, I'll have something to say about that,* Jeff thought.

Again Haynes spoke, "How many muskets ya got this trip?"

"Hundred on the small wagon. A hundred fifty on the big one. Four bags of shot and four of black powder."

"Wow! That's a haul. Does the kid know about it, Kittle?"

"Naw, I kept him working all the time and the bags of grain fooled him. Say, where'd ya tell them Mohawks to meet us?"

"About seven miles from here at Langerd's place."

Jeff strained his ears to catch more, but the men lowered their voices. His heart thumped like a mule stomping at deer flies. Already plans for escape filled his mind. *So that's why the oxen had so much trouble with the heavy wagons, and that must be why Kittle was so positive the Indians wouldn't bother him. When they fall off to sleep tonight I'll make a break for it. The best thing is to get back to Stiles'. I'll work there until someone else comes along headed west. Then I'll join them,* he thought.

The men stirred, their cowhide boots rustled last fall's leaves. Jeff supposed they were preparing for the night. He waited breathlessly. The steps drew near; then a savage kick in the back brought him to his feet. He tried to dodge away into the darkness, but both Kittle and Haynes pinned him down.

"I had a sneakin' idea you was not sleepin'," Haynes snarled.

Too late, Jeff realized he shouldn't have attempted to bolt away then. He should have opened his eyes lazy like in surprise and wonder.

"Well, I'm glad we woke ya up from yer sound sleep," Kittle's voice thickened with sarcasm. "We'll just tie ya up fer the night and see that yer around at sunup."

A heavy rope of smelly rawhide was used to bind his arms and legs securely. "Jake, let's toss him on the wagon. Then if he attempts to wiggle out of them ropes he'll topple off and we'll hear him."

"Good idea," Haynes agreed, and the two men hoisted Jeff to the wagon, putting him so close to the edge that there was danger of the slightest move sending him six feet to the hard stony trail.

The men returned to the fire and rolled in their blankets, content their captive would not get away. Jeff did not sleep at all that night. He lay still, trying to plot some scheme for escape. When a flock of red-winged blackbirds squabbled in the swamp reeds along the river the next morning he was still thinking.

"Looks like our driver is still with us," Haynes laughed when he awoke Kittle.

Kittle untied Jeff with a sharp warning, "If you make one move I don't like, this musket will do my talking and I can tell you me and Jake is the best shots in the valley, ain't we, Jake?"

For an answer, Jake took his musket, aimed it at one of the blackbirds and fired. The gun barked and the blackbird toppled from its perch on the swamp reed. The crooked-nosed man's thin lips parted in a vicious smile. "Guess that'll learn ya how good I am," he laughed.

Jeff was ordered to drive the smaller wagon ahead of

the other. Jake and Kittle both laid their guns on their laps, ready for instant use.

Kittle said, "Jake, I guess this'll be my last trip. I've made enough to get me a little farm up near Niagara."

"What if the settlers win this revolution?" Jake suggested.

"They won't. The British is bound to wipe them out."

"I dunno, there's some that's favorin' George Washington to pull them out from the losing side," Jake Haynes insisted.

"Never!" snorted Kittle. "Why, if Washington should go through another winter like he did at Valley Forge there'd never be another battle fought. If there was half a chance fer the settlers to win do you suppose a man like Benedict Arnold would've turned traitor and swung to the English?"

"Maybe not, but with my money I'm going up to Canada where it's safer. Too many of the settlers suspect me."

On and on they talked, until Jake asked, "Say, Kittle, how much are you giving me fer my part in this job?"

"I figured two hundred dollars would be a fair price," Kittle replied.

"Two hundred!" Jake hissed. "While I stand by and see you clear eight hundred! I want more'n that. After all, I made the arrangements fer them redskins to meet us at Langerd's place. That took some risk."

"Two hundred's all yer gittin'," Kittle insisted.

"Look, Kittle, I'm not riskin' my neck fer that price. We go fifty-fifty, or else—"

Jeff turned around to see Jake Haynes shove the heavy musket into Kittle's ribs. The fat man whined, "Now, Jake, don't git hasty. Let's talk peaceable like. No use in gittin' riled."

"How much you goin' to give me?" Jake insisted.

Jeff waited no longer. Quietly he slipped from the

wagon and leaped into the woods, circling around behind the wagons. A full minute passed before he heard an explosive angry cry of Kittle. "Now, Haynes, look what ya went and done! Let that kid escape."

Down a gully, through a birch grove and over a rocky knoll Jeff raced. He felt reasonably sure the traitors wouldn't risk returning for him, but at each step he felt better.

Traveling as fast as he could he reached the village of Oatfield before noontime. Mr. and Mrs. Stiles were busy at the candle mold when he burst through the door.

"Well, I never expected to see you so soon," Mr. Stiles said, scraping off the wax which stuck to his fingers.

"Last night I heard Kittle and Haynes planning to sell me to the English. They caught me listening, tied me up and then this morning made me drive one of the carts while they followed, covering me with their muskets. I found out those wagons were loaded down with muskets, shot and powder hidden under the bags of grain. They're planning to sell them to the Mohawks at a place called Langerd's. Well, we hadn't gone far when they got to arguing about how the money would be split up. I took a chance when they were squabbling and ducked into the woods and here I am," Jeff panted.

"I knew those two ruffians were up to some low scheme!" Mr. Stiles pounded his fist angrily on the counter, "If only I'd known what was under those bags of grain we could've had them bottled up and packed off to prison at Albany."

Mr. Stiles hurried from the store to the stockade and returned within minutes with a band of men. When they heard what had happened, their fury mounted high.

"Maybe we can get to them before they reach Langerd's place," the red rooster man roared. "Them oxen can't travel too fast driving loads like that."

With Jeff leading the way, nine men took the trail. It was a good three hours before they came upon Langerd's abandoned cabin. Langerd had turned traitor, joining with the English to fight against the settlers.

"Here's the wagon tracks leading north," Mr. Stiles said, pointing to the ruts in the soft mud. They followed for a quarter of a mile when the red rooster man, whose real name was Bud Hurley, called, "We're too late! Look!"

Jeff saw the oxcarts standing off the narrow trail, wrecked. Their wheels were broken and their tops battered so badly that they were useless.

"Moccasin tracks," announced Mr. Stiles, studying the ground. "They met at least twenty redskins here. I suppose they divided up the guns so they could make better time. They probably figured on us chasing them."

Bud Hurley brushed his red topknot back, but it popped straight up when he took his hand away. "You suppose there's any use in taking after them?"

"No. Anyway, they outnumber us and I wouldn't want to get ambushed by a band of Mohawks with as many guns as they have," Mr. Stiles said.

"Nuthin' to do then but go home, aye?" red rooster Bud questioned.

"Probably be better, especially if them Indians decide to raid us." So the men returned without the traitors.

On the way back to Oatfield Jeff felt Mr. Stiles thin, gnarled hand rest on his shoulder. "Well, Jeff, it looks as though you'll be working for me after all."

"I would like to," Jeff said, "but I can't promise how long I'll stay. I'm moving west with the first traveler that comes along."

The new moon lighted the village when Jeff was shown to the loft above the store. "You will find this corn husk mattress mighty comfortable after all the traveling you've done today," Mr. Stiles said, holding a candle for light.

Jeff did just that; he found it so comfortable he fell asleep as soon as his weary head hit the pillow.

3

"Not For Them Fearing Death"

THE DULL STOMPING of heavy boots on the floor below awakened Jeff long before dawn the following morning. He dressed hurriedly, found the ladder in the dark, and climbed downstairs to see Mr. and Mrs. Stiles starting the fire on the hearthstone in back of the store.

"Good morning, Jeff," Mrs. Stiles greeted him as he appeared in the flickering circle of firelight.

"What can I do to help?" he asked.

Mr. Stiles nodded towards the door, "Bring in a few oak chunks for this fire. You'll find them just outside."

Jeff complied, returning with an armful. Mrs. Stiles said, "Now you just sit down, Jeff. I'll have breakfast ready in a few minutes."

Jeff squatted by the fire and watched the prancing shadows caper about on the chinked log walls.

"I'm sorry about your not getting westward to trace your Dad," Mrs. Stiles said, beating honey into the biscuit batter, "but I'm glad you're back with us."

Mr. Stiles added, "It's glad I am that you managed to get away from Kittle and Haynes before you landed in the hands of the Mohawks."

Jeff smiled, "It would surely seem the Lord was traveling with me."

"It would that," Mrs. Stiles agreed. "As I always say,

22

them that puts their trust in the Lord find He's always there when needed."

"Now let me have my say," Mr. Stiles broke in. "Jeff, I've been doing a heap of thinking since we talked last evening. I don't think there's much use of your planning to travel the valley this spring. That Mohawk warrior, Joseph Brant, has already plundered a number of settlements and I heard a rumor that Johnson and Butler, those two English generals, plan to wipe the settlers out this summer. Travelers risking passage have been taken time after time, for wagon ruts are easy to follow." Mr. Stiles leaned forward and tapped Jeff's knee with a long crooked finger, "My idea is this now, Jeff, you just plan to stay on here with us until the war's over. The chances of finding your father will be a heap better then, I'm thinking."

Sarah Stiles turned from the fire and looked at Jeff, "Four years ago our boy, just a mite older than you, joined the militia and was killed when Herkimer defeated St. Leger at Oriskany." She continued softly, "Jeff, Will and me would like to have you take his place."

For a long time Jeff stared blankly into the fire. Many thoughts flashed through his mind, *What lies westward? Indians — burning — killing — hating — maybe death for me? And yet, somewhere out there I'll find my father. Perhaps dead. Maybe alive. Perhaps a prisoner of the English.*

The troubling questions were like savage whip lashes, goading him on. Jeff was not conscious of the paling light filtering through the haze to the east, flooding the valley with dawn; nor was he aware of the old couple as they studied him. Outside, cows driven from the stockade towards pasture, tinkled the musical bells around their necks as they walked. The big shepherd dog thumped his tail, suddenly rose to his feet, raced out the door and barked at the cattle as he was used to doing every morning.

Only then did Jeff look up. He spent the next half

hour telling the Stiles of his home in Albany. He described the tiny bakery shop and how his mother and sister were doing the work until he brought back word. He told of his ambition to settle some day in the Mohawk Valley and build a cabin for himself and farm the fertile ground.

"I'm pleased with your offer," he concluded, "but my mind's made up. It's westward I'm going at the first opportunity."

"Jeff," Mr. Stiles plucked idly at his beard, "Jeff, we're going to hate to see you go, but between now and that time, make this your home. Take your meals with us; sleep upstairs, and I'll give you a dollar a week for helping me out in the store."

Jeff was glad for this kindness. That very morning he began helping the old man. While dusting off the shelves he wondered how long it would be before he could continue westward again along the Mohawk River. Though he knew it was the better part of good judgment to wait for a caravan, yet he set June 1 as the deadline. If no one came through by then he would go alone, no matter what. That meant at the most thirty days working for Mr. Stiles.

After a busy morning cleaning and waiting on the various settlers who came in for supplies, Mr. Stiles said, "Jeff, take the afternoon off. Go over to the stockade and get acquainted. There's a scout over there by the name of Carl Ives you should meet. He's probably the best woodsman in New York territory. I heard he arrived early this morning. Besides, if an Indian raid should come, that would be your home for a while."

His attention was focused on the stockade. It stood upon the northern ridge of the valley, holding a commanding view of the river front and all the cabins. Made of huge logs driven into the ground, it looked like some great weird ship. Each log was sharpened to a point at the top, extending about twelve feet into the air, to forestall any attempt to scale the barrier.

The stockade was built in a circular fashion and covered a good half acre of ground. Within the outer framework of timbers Jeff saw the blockhouse, a square log building rising above the level of the barrier. A three-foot ramp led around this, enabling a man to move from one spot to another. As he drew close Jeff could see widened cracks between the logs. These were loopholes through which the settlers could fire their muskets in case of a raid.

An armed man hailed him at the gate, "I'm not familiar with you, boy!" he challenged.

"I'm Jeff Lockwood, working at Stiles store for the time being."

"I thought so. I heard of your close call with Kittle and Haynes. I never did trust that pair. It's just as well we know their true colors now." That man tapped his gun barrel significantly, "Well, as long as you've proven yourself I guess you can poke around."

Jeff smiled as he entered. He was surprised to see three other buildings beside the blockhouse within the fort. One was long and low. Not a window showed. This, he imagined rightly, was the place where the women folk and babies huddled during an attack. The other building was open on one side with hay stored at the back for the cows, horses and sheep. The last building, by far the smallest, was filled with log benches facing a platform. *Where they hold their worship services,* thought Jeff, spying a Bible placed on a tree trunk cut low for a pulpit.

The blockhouse beckoned him. It looked lonely and frightening because of what it brought to his mind — red warriors, faces painted with fruit, nut and clay dyes creeping close to kill.

He pushed open a leather-hinged door and saw muskets standing along the log wall in the dim light. A ladder led upward to the loft where a low opening gave passageway to the ramp outside. Coming to the second floor he looked out towards the river. The spring sun turned it into a broad ribbon of flowing silver. The figures of the grazing stock looked like toys in the distance. The men and women in the fields were midgets; the dogs were like mice. He shifted to the far side and saw the endless stretch of forest billowing away to the north in green waves.

A small opening led outside to the ledge. The view was better from there. Jeff imagined the hordes of Indians roaming the woods sweeping upon the stockade. He wondered if the war would ever cease. *Would the people ever again be able to live in peace, or would the threat of raids always line their faces and chill their hearts with fear?*

"Hello, there!" The unexpected greeting startled Jeff so badly he stumbled backwards as he whirled about to face a towering frontiersman leaning against the blockhouse with one foot resting on the guard rail.

"'Guess I caught you unprepared, didn't I?" the stranger laughed.

"Yes, sir," Jeff stuttered.

The fringed, buff colored, buckskin jacket covered broad, massive shoulders and hard muscled arms. Soft buckskin breeches covered long legs to where they met cowhide moccasins, each patterned with an eagles wing.

More than anything else, however, it was the man's face that arrested Jeff's interest. Never had he seen a face like it, black hair, glistening like a raven's breast, fell to the fringed shoulder pads; keen eyes, dark as charred oak, peered from under shaggy brows, and the clean shaven face was in sharp contrast to the bearded faces which were common habit among the men of the day.

"Here, squat down a while and talk with me. It gets a bit lonesome just watching for redskins." The man moved his musket to make room for Jeff to sit with his back against the wall.

"Now, then, you're Jefferson Lockwood, late from

Albany and out here in the Mohawk Valley in search of your father, who's been missing for over a year. At the present you're working for Brother Stiles at the store, and you're about as restless as a hungry trout at feeding time."

"You seem to have me tagged about perfect," Jeff grinned, puzzled.

"Well, that red-headed fellow, Bud Hurley, got a hold of my ear and caught me up with all the news at Oatfield."

"You must be the scout, Carl Ives."

"Right, Jeff." The man left Jeff's side for a moment and looped around the ramp on all four sides and returned. "Things are quiet. I'm glad. It gives the men a chance to get their seed in."

"It's hard to believe danger is so close," Jeff said.

"It is," the scout agreed. "Oatfield has not been touched up to now. This is a strong place with at least thirty men who know how to shoot, so the English haven't molested us yet. And the Indians are too wary. But bad days are coming, and when they do, those cabins down there will be smouldering ashes, I'm afraid."

The sobering words made Jeff thoughtful. "Is it really as bad as I've heard? I mean about the Indian raids and the English slaughtering the settlers?"

"It's worse. It's terrible Jeff, and for one, I'll be glad when it's over."

Jeff found it easy to tell this tall, slender quick-moving man about his search for his father.

Carl Ives rose to his feet when Jeff finished, towering over the boy. "Jeff, I don't blame you none for wanting word. It's right that you should go, but you might find heartbreak out there with the answer to your question about your Dad." The scout looked troubled. Somehow Jeff felt this man knew more than he would admit. Perhaps he had word of his father's capture, or even death. Before he could push the questioning further Carl Ives cradled the musket in the crook of his arm and looked down at him. "Jeff," his face was drawn with seriousness, "are you a Christian? I don't mean one who says he is, but ain't. I mean, do you know the Lord down deep here?" he tapped his chest suggestively. "Do you know you have life beyond the one you now have?"

Jeff looked at the penetrating eyes; the earnest voice drilled deep within him. He remembered the meeting back in Albany and how relieved he felt when he found himself believing the work of salvation finished by Christ.

"Yes, sir. I believe. I'm a Christian," he replied.

"It will do well by you. If you weren't, I'd say go home. This place is not for them fearing death."

At that moment the red rooster man, Bud Hurley, came to relieve Carl Ives. "Look, I have to do a little scouting. I want to check those hills yonder before nightfall, but come back. There's something I have worth telling you. Come back after dusk. I'll be up here."

The man swung down the ladder and without a sound padded across the stockade, out the gate, and toward the distant hills, already shadowed purple as the sun eased beyond the forest. A sudden longing welled up in Jeff. A longing to be a scout. But more than that, to be a scout like Carl Ives.

Bud Hurley nodded towards the disappearing figure, "The finest Christian man I ever met. A body feels safe when he's around."

4

"There's Danger Out There!"

A CRACKLING FIRE by the gate lighted the stockade when Jeff walked from Stiles' store to keep his appointment with Carl Ives. Bud Hurley, his red hair flashing in the flame glow, squatted beside a gaunt, frontiersman.

"Hello, there Jeff!" Bud called. "Sit ya down by the fire a while."

"I came over to talk with Carl Ives."

"He ain't back yet, but he'll be amblin' in 'fore long, so you might as well sit."

Jeff hunkered down on a length of cord wood as Bud asked, "You know Carl real well?"

"No, this afternoon was the first time I ever laid eyes on him."

"You could learn heaps from him. There's not a better man in the woods. It always has been a mystery to me how he can slip through the wilderness so still-like, being as big as he is; moves quiet as a feather fallin' on snow, and can go for hours on end without tiring."

The other man, his face almost as narrow as a shingle, added, "I talked to an Indian last week over Holme's way. A Tuscarora he was, and he tells me that this here Carl Ives you're speaking of is better than the Indians themselves when it comes to huntin' and trackin'."

"Aren't the Tuscarora's the enemies of the settlers?" Jeff asked rather surprised.

"Naw, them's real friendly like. Them and the Oniedas aren't fightin' with the English agin' us."

Bud Hurley explained, "You see, Jeff, there's six different bands of redskins in this here York state territory. Together they form the Iroquois. The two tribes Tog just mentioned are friendly with us settlers. It's the other four tribes that gives us heaps of worry. There's nuthin' worse than a band of raiding Mohawks or the slinky Seneca's. They're a crafty lot. I ain't sayin' as how I blame them much, seein' their land's taken and seein' the white man cheats them of furs and other things. But I don't like them. I've seen too many burned-out homes. I reckon this year, 1780, will go down in history as the bloodiest there ever was in these parts."

Shingle-face tossed another oak chunk on the fire, sending up a shower of sparks. "Carl Ives has heaps of friends among all the tribes, yet he's afeared of coming raids."

Shep, Mr. Stiles' dog, walked up and touched Jeff's face with his cold nose. Jeff reached out to pat him when the hair began to raise along the dog's back. A deep, rumbling growl sounded in his chest.

A voice, surprisingly close, came from the darkness beyond the log gate. "Bud Hurley, sound the alarm for gathering. I think we're in for trouble!"

Without a question Bud leaped to his feet and raced to the Stockade, his heavy boots telling his path. The thin man was on his feet when Carl Ives came into the circle of firelight. "What be the matter?" he questioned.

"'Spotted fifteen Mohawks camped seven miles west of here. They're painted for war and headed this way from the looks of things. We can't take any risks."

At that moment a long blast from a horn echoed and re-echoed from atop the blockhouse. Almost immediately shouting could be heard from the nearby cabins, as the people rushed to get to the stockade for safety. Again and again the weird horn blasted its warning cry. Soon settlers began to pass the gate. Jeff saw the Stiles enter, both of them carrying muskets. Behind them a man and woman followed by nine children trooped in.

Ten minutes passed when a man at the gate called, "Everyone from Oatfield is accounted for!"

Carl Ives mounted a wagon and stood on the seat, "Friends," he shouted, "I've had the horn sounded because I saw Mohawks in paint headed this way. I'm not certain it's a raid, but we'll take no chances. The men are to take their regular places. Single women will stand on hand to load muskets. No one shall talk, and all fires out."

The mothers, with their children, found shelter in the long cabin. Jeff saw their taut, worried faces as they went by the fire. A baby began to cry in fear and the mother's soft reassuring tones sounded loud against the silence of the night.

Jeff stood near the fire uncertainly for a few moments when Carl came over and scattered the embers with his foot, "Jeff, you come along with me, I might be able to use you."

In the gloom of night Jeff followed Carl Ives' broad back past the building where the women could be heard settling their children for the night, to the blockhouse where they mounted the ladder to the outside ramp.

The shadowy figures of the men were barely visible against the sky. Just the occasional cough or shuffle of feet on the logs, or the murmur of whispers could be heard. There was a tenseness in the air that Jeff had never before experienced. The darkness hemmed them in from all sides; not a star glimmered above.

Carl Ives breathed close to his ear, "Jeff, we'll take this westward side. Squat down and keep your ears and eyes open. If you hear anything nudge me."

He stared into the gloom. The man stationed ten feet

to the right blew his nose so loud Jeff almost jumped, he was so startled. A fox yapped away off on a distant hill; another answered from the south beyond the Mohawk River.

Bud Hurley's voice called in a carrying whisper, "Carl, could that be a signal?"

"No, it's the real thing." Carl returned.

An owl hooted from atop the blockhouse again and again. "That thing's gettin' on my nerves," a man growled half aloud and then tossed a sliver of bark at the bird. The soft whir-r-r-r of wings drifted down as the barred owl flew away.

"That's better," the man's voice sounded as though his head were in a barrel.

A cold damp wind whisked from the east; a raindrop spattered on Jeff's forehead, then another, and another. Bud Hurley whispered, "Rain! Just the kind of weather them warriors like, makes their footsteps absolutely silent."

"Watch careful," Carl warned.

Jeff wondered how any sort of a defense could possibly be made. He couldn't see the nearest cabin, in fact, the stockade itself was a blank. He found himself talking to the Lord, asking Him to take care of the women and children huddled below. He thought of his father, his mother and sister.

An unexpected shout clamored from the southwest corner of the blockhouse. "Look! There's Kendal's place going up in flames!" Jeff saw the fire strangely bright, about three miles off, glowing like a torch against the sky. A wave of terror swept through him. "Mr. Ives," he asked, "are the Kendals in the stockade?"

"No, Jeff. They're out there some place. We can just hope they got away. There's five young ones."

Jeff bit his lips, half in fear and half in anger at the cruelty of the war that raged between the settlers and the English. The distant blaze reached its peak, then lowered and faded from view.

Again silence settled over the men, only the sprinkling patter of drumming rain made any noise. Jeff cocked his head, leaning over the guard rail when he thought he heard a far away shout. *Probably my imagination,* he thought.

But again the sound wafted to his ears. "Mr. Ives, I heard something off to the west. It sounded like a shout."

Carl Ives didn't answer, but a moment later another shout sounded, this time louder and closer. Carl called out, "Someone's coming! It might be the Kendals. Be ready at the gate!"

Ten still minutes, a distant drum of horses hoofs and wagon wheels, a frightened voice crying in the night, "Open up! Open up! There's redskins!"

Carl shouted, "Is that you, Kendal?"

"Yes, Open up!"

Carl called to the man at the gate, "Open up. Kendal's coming!"

Jeff traced the activity from the sounds. The gate creaked open. Horses hoofs thundered in. The gate closed with a noisy bang. A woman sobbed: *Probably Mrs. Kendal,* Jeff thought. Someone asked, "All yer kids all right?"

"All here, thank the good Lord," Mr. Kendal answered. Then silence again. Jeff could hardly breathe from excitement. At any moment he expected to hear the explosive thunder of muskets or the shrieking, hideous scream of attacking redskins.

Mr. Kendal worked his way up the ladder and moved past Jeff to speak to Carl Ives. He said, "I was just beginning to milk the cows when I saw a single brave watching me from behind the big maple tree on my place. I saw him duck back into the woods and figured he was going to tell the others, so I lit out about sundown."

"You figured right. I spotted a roving band to the west," Carl Ives told the man. Then he added, "Say, did you know your house was burned?"

Mr. Kendal's voice filled with despair, "I thought as

much. We couldn't see, for the trees, but I smelled smoke. That'll about break my wife's heart. She'd worked awful hard fixing it up snug and cozy for me and the kids."

Carl circled the blockhouse, telling each man what had happened and warning, "Keep awake. If they followed Kendal they're mighty close now."

The raw wind swirled the rain into Jeff's face as he stared into the night. Suddenly from the east side of the stockade a dog began to bark. A musket exploded.

Carl Ives whispered, "What was that, John?"

Even in the excitement, Jeff wondered how Carl knew who shot, but he proved to be right, for John Barnes answered, "For the last five minutes I've been seeing something moving down there, so when that dog barked I figured it was a Mohawk."

Carl left Jeff's side with the words, "I'm going out to have a look."

More deadly silence. Five minutes dragged like an hour. Ten minutes like six hours. Twenty awful minutes seemed as long as night itself.

Without warning Carl Ives was back laughing softly, "Hey, John! You know what you shot?"

John's voice trembled with tenseness. "A redskin?"

"Nope. But you did get something. It was that pure white cow of yours."

The men laughed and some of the tension broke. Yet, the slow hours between midnight and dawn were tiresome, for every man knew the danger if sleep were to overtake them and allow a sneak raid.

A rooster crowed when morning paled the sky eastward. Below in the long cabin the children began to awaken. A baby cried. The rain stopped and the sun's warm rays slipped through the clouds.

Fires were lit and the woman folk prepared breakfast for the tired men. Everyone laughed when they saw John's cow in the field not far from the fort. It was laughter of relief, for the night of terror was over. Besides, it also meant there would be a feast of steak for everyone.

Most of the men whose cabins were within sight of the stockade risked going out to bring their cows and oxen to safety. But no man went alone. There were always several with him, well armed for fear of ambush.

At midday Carl Ives scouted the country and returned to report that the redskins had bypassed the Oatfield Fort and headed east. He invited Jeff to the ramp for a turn at guarding while some of the men slept.

Carl spoke, "Jeff, last night I wanted to tell you about a missionary and his family coming west from Albany to do Christian work among the settlers and the Indians. Last year Mr. Watson was out here alone and built a cabin for the family. Now that it's done he's returning with them. If everything goes well, they should be passing within two weeks. I plan to go west with them to Fort Killypox. Captain Snow is stationed there and he wants me for scout work in that area. If you want, there'll be room for you to travel with us."

"I'll be with you," Jeff openly showed his enthusiasm at the prospect. Then he felt he must question Carl Ives about his father and asked, "Mr. Ives, do you know anything of my father you haven't told me?"

Carl Ives brushed the long black hair over his shoulders and stared for a moment to the river. Finally he replied, "Jeff, first of all, don't bother calling me Mr. Ives. 'Makes me seem too old. Make it Carl. Then, about your question. For one thing, I believe your father's still alive. Where he is I wouldn't know. Jeff," the scout leaned forward and put a hand on his shoulder, "I've heard lots of things said of men that aren't so. I heard a man say something about your father once, but I didn't believe it, so I won't mention it now.

But, Jeff, whatever comes, put your trust in the Lord and He'll see you through no matter what."

Jeff pushed his questioning, but Carl wouldn't say further what was on his mind. Before sundown Carl said he was going to look over the country before nightfall. Jeff seized the opportunity to ask, "Carl, could I go with you? I want to learn how to track and hunt and all the other things that're needed in this wilderness."

Carl replied, "Well, Jeff, I guess you could, but there's danger out there and I can't say we won't meet it."

Carl led the way westward until they came to the burned heap that had once been a home for the Kendals. Nearby they found three cows slaughtered. The only living things about the scarred embers were a half dozen chickens scratching for food.

They circled back, Carl in the lead, studying the ground for moccasin prints. At dusk when they returned to Oatfield, however, they had nothing to report. Some of the braver settlers went to their homes, rather than stay in the crowded stockade for the night. Jeff, with Mr. and Mrs. Stiles, went to the store.

5

"A Dash For Safety"

"WHAT'S THE FIRST THING you want me to work on this morning, Mr. Stiles?" Jeff asked.

"You'll find a barrel of black powder behind the counter over there. Drag it out and weigh it up into pound sacks."

The spring sun spattered patches of light through a maple tree in front of the store. Shep, the dog, was at his usual place near the doorway sleeping with a half-grown yellow kitten.

Even as Jeff worked there was a restless desire to break away for the Stanwix stockade. *It's funny the way things don't go to a fellow's way of planning all the time,* he thought. First there was Kittle, and the slow plodding oxen dragging the concealed ·muskets. Then, of course, there was his narrow escape, and following that came the scare of Indian raiders.

"Well," Jeff muttered to himself when he stacked the last bag of powder on the shelf above the woolen cloth, "there's not much I can do now but wait. As soon as the missionary and his family arrive I'll be on my way again."

Shep thumped his tail on the floor and raised his nose, sniffing the air. He rose, stretched, barked a few times, and suddenly raced eastward along the trail.

"Well, what do you make of that?" Jeff asked Mr. Stiles.

"Like as not he spotted a squirrel or a cottontail."

Off in the woods they could hear the baying growing fainter and fainter until it seemed to stay in one place. Jeff asked, "Mr. Stiles, could I take your musket and see if I could get whatever he's after?"

"Sure."

Jeff balanced the gun on his arm and moved along the trail. Up ahead Shep's barking increased in volume. Pausing, Jeff heard a rumbling noise.

Soon a wagon, a big loaded affair with three people perched on it, trundled into view. Shep bounced along side, voicing his greeting.

Jeff returned to the store and told Mr. Stiles of the new-comers. "Maybe it's that missionary, Mr. Watson, and his folks. He's got a daughter just a bit younger than you and there's a baby about ten months old, I understand."

The storekeeper came to the door brushing flour from his hands and slapping the white dust from his apron. The wagon rounded the edge of the Oatfield clearing, with Shep still barking his delight. Mr. Stiles waved as he said, "It's them all right. Can you imagine that? They come right through the Indian lines and didn't get touched!"

The driver, a medium tall, sandy-haired man, pulled up the laboring oxen under the maple tree. The woman beside him reminded Jeff of his own mother. She was dark haired, with a flashing quickness about her eyes that made a fellow want to know her better. On her right arm was a tiny baby cradled in a blanket and telling the world with no uncertain bellow that she figured it was feeding time.

Behind the couple sat a girl about a year younger than Jeff's sixteen years. Her honey colored hair fell in two long pigtails over the shoulders of her homespun jacket. Her blue eyes were happily looking at Shep, but even from where he stood Jeff could see she was dead tired from the ride in the jouncing, springless wagon.

"We made it, Mr. Stiles," Mr. Watson laughed, swinging to the ground.

Mrs. Stiles emerged from the door of the store and the next few moments were given over to hearty welcomes. Jeff stood to one side in great expectancy. Soon now the westward trail would be feeling his footsteps.

Carl Ives came over from the stockade and greeted the newcomers. He turned to Jeff, "Jeff, meet the Watsons. You'll be seeing them aplenty for a goodly space of time. This here baby's name is Pam, and that sprite of a girl petting Shep is Maud."

Maud tossed a troublesome pigtail over her shoulder and flashed a blue-eyed smile. With introductions over, Jeff busied himself tending the oxen and seeing to the wagon. The Watsons washed up behind the store and ate the abundant dinner Mrs. Stiles whipped up, then they were off to bed to sleep on mattresses for the first time in almost two weeks.

They arose, refreshed, before supper. Carl ate with them and the conversation swung to plans for leaving. Mr. Watson spoke, "Well, Carl, there's my land out beyond Killypox waiting for the seed, so I think the earlier we lift stakes the better."

"Suits me right fine," Carl agreed. "Captain Snow wants me at Killypox for a while and Jeff here is boiling to find his father."

"We'll leave in the morning, then," decided Mr. Watson.

Word had passed around the fort about the missionary's arrival and immediate plans were laid for a service in the chapel. It wasn't often a preacher was available and the place was crowded with just about everyone within traveling distance.

Mr. Watson opened his Bible to the Twenty-Third Psalm and read it. Then earnestly he repeated the fourth verse. "Yea, though I walk through the valley of the shadow of death, I will fear no evil: for Thou art with me; Thy rod and Thy staff they comfort me.

"The Mohawk Valley has been the valley of the shadow of death for the last four long years. Blood has poured from the men and women who tried to establish a nation free from the tyranny of England. This is important, yet there is something more important. It's that great fight for the freedom of a man's soul. This freedom can be won only by putting your faith in the Lord Jesus Christ who gave his life to free us from the bondage of sin."

Jeff listened attentively and he saw the other settlers leaning forward harking to every phrase. They, indeed, had seen the terror of the night and many of them had put their trust in the Lord.

When the sermon ended the people gathered in little groups and talked. Jeff stood near Mr. Watson, Carl Ives and red rooster Bud Hurley. Another man, the one with the shingle face, came up to them.

He showed open disapproval, "Say, there, Preacher Watson, I don't line up with you on all ya said. Seems to me that the Lord oughta' be a bit more easy on us folks out here. Besides, I can't see that one man like the Lord Jesus Christ could save everybody if they just believe on Him."

Mr. Watson's voice was gentle and quiet. "Do you think it's foolishness to fight for the freedom of our nation?"

"No, but that's different."

"Perhaps, but there is something similar. If this nation is to be free, men have to die; blood must be shed. Now, there is a battle waging for every man's soul. The devil wants it, and the Lord wants it. The only way for spiritual freedom comes by the death of Christ. He gave his life to win the battle for every man who will believe in Him."

The thin face grew sharp and hard. Mr. Watson pressed the point, "Perhaps something I saw up in Vermont territory a few years ago will illustrate my point. There was a terrible forest fire in one section and after the fire died out I happened to be walking over the burned out land when I spotted a dead mother partridge crumpled on the ground with her feathers burned. I picked her up and to my surprise I found seven chicks under her, all alive and safe. She had given her life for the chicks' salvation. If that partridge had not sacrificed her life those little chicks would've been destroyed. In a way that's what the Lord Jesus did for us. Those that spurn the safety of Christ will perish."

The bitterness of unbelief still lined the thin man's face when he walked away, but for Jeff, Mr. Watson's words helped him understand just a bit better what the Lord had done for him.

The dew wet grass soaked Jeff's bare feet the next morning when he led the yoke of oxen in from the pasture land. The wagon readied for leaving, he returned to Stiles' store where the Watsons had spent the night. A lump of sadness tugged at his heart when he thought of leaving the old folks who had taken him in as their own son, but the constant whiplash of desire made him yearn to get going.

Carl Ives helped Maud on the wagon and tossed his small bundle to her. Jeff had lost his belongings when he escaped from Kittle and Haynes. Mr. Watson had given him a blanket, a leather-sheathed hunting knife and a musket with powder and shot, but outside of these items he had nothing but the clothes he wore.

Goodbyes were said, and the wagon rumbled off along the river trail.

Carl and Jeff walked ahead. A deep throated 'gugerrum' thundered from the marsh along the river as a bullfrog greeted the new day. Another answered, and still another, until the river echoed with the strange bass music. A muskrat, startled by the two men, splashed into the water.

The trail rambled along the river, sometimes to cling to

the very edge of the water, sometimes curving away to round a swamp or high flung ledge of shaley rock. Carl's moccasined feet were nearly silent, but Jeff's cowhide boots scraped and clattered with a fearful racket. Try as he might to imitate Carl's easy stride, toes pointed ahead, touching the ground lightly with every step, he still made noise.

"Jeff, the first chance we get, let's change those clumsy boots for a pair of moccasins."

"I guess I make a lot of racket," Jeff admitted ruefully.

"I'm afraid you wouldn't do as a scout with those things."

At noon they stopped to eat and rest an hour. Maud and Jeff gathered firewood. Maud said, "I'm glad you and Carl are with us. It was rather scareful at night when we were alone."

"I'm going west in search of my father," Jeff explained.

"I know, I heard Mr. Stiles telling Dad. I hope you find him."

"I hope so too. It's been over a year now."

Jeff told her all about his narrow escape from Kittle and Haynes. When he finished Maud said, "This is my first trip. Dad came out last summer and built a cabin near Killypox. He stayed for the winter clearing land for spring planting. He came for us a couple of weeks ago."

"Someday I hope to have a farm out here."

"I kind of like it," Maud continued, "it's so wild and quiet, but there's been times when I get homesick for my friends back in Albany."

"But someday there'll be cities out here. If the war is won thousands of people will settle in this territory. There's heaps of land just for the clearing."

After the meal the pioneers pushed on again. It was a day and a half later when they arrived at a tiny settlement of three cabins. Here Carl swapped Jeff's boots for a tanned deerhide. He cut the leather, using Jeff's foot as a guide for the pattern. Before they pulled away, the new moccasins were finished and Jeff's woodsman training began in earnest.

Together they forged far ahead of the wagon, Carl pointing out the little things that told hundreds of stories about wood life; Jeff listened and wondered if he could ever learn all the things experience had taught the scout.

Time after time Jeff grew disgusted when he would be easing his way forward, only to spoil it all by treading on a dry twig or blundering into an overhanging limb. Carl would laugh and say, "You're doing far better than I expected. Keep at it; never forget your action in the woods may mean your life."

Then there were the tracks. Once near the edge of the river Carl stopped and pointed to the soft earth, "See, Jeff, there's where a deer came to drink; a doe I'd judge by the narrowness of the hoofs. Yes, see here, the tracks of her fawn." Jeff studied the ground and after a struggle saw what the scout had seen in a flash. As the time passed he found it a bit easier; he began to recognize coon, skunk, beaver, muskrats, fox and many other animal tracks.

One evening after supper he told Carl, "I'm going upstream a ways to practice tracking. I'll take along a fish line and maybe catch a few trout for breakfast."

He caught two trout and saw a wide mud flat a hundred yards away. Figuring it a good place to fish, he worked his way toward it. The soft mud showed countless tracks. Here a raccoon hunted for frogs. There a large blue heron had fished, his long toes making a huge pattern. A deer had come to drink; the tracks showed where it stood and tested the wind before it lowered its head.

A large imprint caught his eye. *Bear,* he thought. *No, wait — that's not bear, there's no claw prints. That's a moccasin track! An Indian track, and freshly made. Now to get back to camp. Carl will want to see it. Darkness is closing in. Have to hurry!* And hurry he did.

Within twenty minutes he was back pointing out the track to Carl. The scout took one glance, "He's mighty close. Look, the water's just beginning to ooze in the track. You probably missed seeing him by minutes."

They followed the track for a quarter of a mile, then the light faded and they returned to camp. Carl covered the fire with sod. "That will keep the smoke from telling where we are, that is, if they don't already know."

"How many do you think there are?" questioned Mr. Watson.

"We can't tell yet, but the trail we followed was probably made by one of their scouts. The first thing in the morning I'll circle camp and pick up the trail and see what's at the other end." Carl said, "Jeff, tie the oxen to that tree near the wagon. No use letting them thrash around making a lot of noise. We can spread the blankets under the wagon for the night. I just hope Pam picks this night to sleep real good. Nothing carries like a baby's crying."

A clammy dampness rolled in from the river at midnight and within an hour a gentle rain began to fall. Sleep wasn't for the wilderness travelers that evening. They huddled under the wagon and talked in whispers.

Jeff asked, "Mr. Watson, there's something I'd like to get straightened out. Maybe you could explain it to me."

"Be glad to, Jeff. What is it?"

"Well, just after I accepted the Lord Jesus Christ back in Albany, I began to wonder just what would happen if I were to die, so I asked a woman and she told me that when we die we don't know anything for years and years. We just lay in the grave until the day of resurrection."

Mr. Watson snorted in displeasure, "Jeff, that woman didn't know her Bible."

"Well, suppose that Indian we tracked knew we were

here and reported back to his band and led them to us. Just suppose we were killed, just what would happen?"

"Jeff, if that were to happen this very night a most wonderful thing would occur. We would immediately be in the presence of the Lord Jesus Christ."

"You mean we wouldn't lose consciousness?" Jeff asked.

"That's right. We would be conscious all the time. The Bible tells us, the man who accepted Christ on the Cross asked to be remembered when He arrived in the kingdom. Remember the Lord's answer? 'Verily I say unto thee, Today shalt thou be with Me in paradise.' Actually while death is unpleasant because it means separation from loved ones, there really is nothing to fear for the Christian, no matter what happens."

"Thanks, Mr. Watson. That clears things up a bit," Jeff said.

Maud added, "If it weren't for knowing that, I'd be scared to death out here in this awful darkness, knowing Indians were nearby."

At dawn Carl Ives left the camp and drifted off into the woods to scout the trail ahead. Within an hour he returned, his face revealing knowledge, unpleasant knowledge, for lines of worry showed plainly.

"I found them, nine in all. They have a camp two miles west. That means they're between us and the Killypox stockade."

"How many miles is the stockade from here?" Mr. Watson asked.

"About four miles."

"Could we risk a dash for safety?" Jeff questioned.

"They'd find us for sure. I thought of going through to get help, but the danger's too great. They might pick up my trail and back track to this camp. I think we'd better stay right here, waiting and praying."

D

6

"The Biggest Job You Ever Had"

"IN A WAY I'M GLAD it's raining. Those wagon tracks we left on the trail would be easy picking for any redskin to follow. With this downpour they'll be wiped out," Carl commented, watching a little river of water running down the rim of the wheel.

"The thing that surprises me is how quiet Pam has been. I'd hate to hear her burst into tears. Those redmen could hear her a mile away," Jeff held the baby girl close and gave her a generous hug.

Carl took a leather pouch of bear grease from his sack and rubbed his buckskin jacket for waterproofing. He said, "I think I'll have another look at the Indian camp. I'd sure like to get to Killypox Stockade before they find us."

The scout put on a beaverskin hat and stepped into the rain, to disappear a moment later behind a witch hazel bush. Jeff felt a surge of disappointment bother him, for he had hoped Carl would take him along. He thought, "Just proves I'm as clumsy as an ox. I'll have to practice and practice until I can move as quiet as he can."

Within an hour the scout returned, running hard. "Hurry, hitch up! We're moving!"

Jeff leaped to the oxen, sensing the urgency of the orders. As he adjusted the yoke Carl explained, "They broke camp and headed north. If we move fast we can probably make Killypox without trouble."

The trail was good, the oxen fresh, and fast time was made. Jeff trotted with Carl beside the swaying wagon, "Jeff," the scout said, "if those warriors had found us we'd know now what death was like. They are on the war trail."

"How much further, Carl?" Mr. Watson called from the wagon.

"About three miles more! I think I'll drop back a ways and make certain they aren't following. Jeff, you go ahead a quarter of a mile. Keep your eyes open."

Jeff widened the gap between him and the wagon. *At least the muddy trail muffles my footsteps,* he thought, eyeing every tree and bush suspiciously for signs of an ambush. "What was that?" Jeff stopped and harkened to the noise. Faraway he heard Carl's voice calling, "Jeff! Jeff!"

Wheeling about, he let his long legs fly. The wagon came into view, the oxen laboring to match Mr. Watson's excited voice.

"Climb up, Jeff!" Carl shouted from his perch beside the driver.

Jeff leaped on, drawing himself over the side, "What's the matter?" he panted.

"They found our camp and picked up the trail. One of them saw me."

A sloping hill slowed the animals. Their black hides were flecked with foam. "We'll never make it," Carl moaned.

Almost as the words were spoken a shrill scream drifted from a half mile behind them. Mrs. Watson held Pam close. Maud's white face showed terror, but no cry escaped her lips. Jeff felt a strange sensation sweep over him. Anger, fear or excitement, he wasn't sure which.

Mr. Watson smiled wanly, "Now is when our Christianity is tested. We must center our trust in the Lord. He worked miracles when He walked upon the earth and His arm is still mighty and powerful. Let us look to Him for help in this hour."

The oxen dragged the wagon over the rise and made better speed down hill. Again from behind them came hideous screams from the war-crazed redskins.

Suddenly Carl snapped his fingers, "There's a chance, Jeff, I'm going to give you the biggest job you ever had."

Jeff nodded wonderingly.

"See, below in the valley. There's a stream. We'll stop in the middle of it. Mr. Watson, you lift down your wife. Maud, you scramble for yourself. I'll take the baby, but don't make any tracks on the bank. Then, Jeff, you drive those oxen for all you're worth. Keep to the trail and when you see Killypox shout louder than you ever did before so they'll open the gate for the team. If the redskins fall for the trick they'll bypass us and give us time to escape. If they catch up with you, take to your heels. I know you can outrun them."

There was no chance for more talk. The oxen halted and already Mr. Watson was over the side with his wife. Carl plunged into the waistdeep water with Pam. Maud slid down the canvas with a swishing splash.

Carl gave the nearest oxen a wallop with the palm of his hand and the animals lunged forward. A scream echoed wildly through the woods and Jeff knew the Indians were gaining.

Rain splashed his cheeks, creeping in chilly riverlets down his collar to pool up where his belt blocked the way. He glanced at the canvassed wagon. All the Watsons' belongings were under there. "The three window frames all the way from Albany," Jeff muttered aloud. "Mrs. Watson's little organ. Maud's favorite cream pitcher from her aunt in Holland. And Pam's rag doll."

Pam's rag doll! Jeff half smiled, thinking of the comical eyes Maud had stitched on the calico face. Then, there were the hundred Bibles and the hymn books. If the

Indians managed to get the wagon all would be lost. The troublesome thought drove Jeff to prayer.

Only the "Amen" was spoken aloud. "It's funny I haven't heard them shriek the last few minutes." Alarm flooded him, "What if they found Carl and the Watsons!"

In dismay Jeff twisted on the board seat and looked back along the trail. Only the drenched woods met his view. He was about to slow the oxen when he heard the war cry. He saw one bronze warrior swing toward him a quarter of a mile away. The Indian stopped and raised a long barreled musket. The shot cut the leaves above Jeff's head. The Mohawk reloaded and the oxen gained a hundred yards.

Jeff took the leather whip from its socket and snapped it above the oxen. The warrior kneeled again and another shot rattled through the trees off to the right. With a scream, the redskin tossed the rifle into the brush and apparently disgusted with the white man's weapon tugged a tomahawk from his belt. He leaped forward and Jeff saw the gap close.

Far behind two more Indians appeared. The leading runner screamed again. At the sound one of the oxen bellowed with terror thrashing sideways, almost upsetting the wagon. Jeff dragged with all his strength on the line and barely managed to steady the fear-crazed animal.

Jeff got ready to leap and take to his heels as Carl had suggested. But up ahead he saw an opening through the trees. "If that's Killypox maybe I can make it yet." With that hope he abandoned the idea of trying to race the redskins on foot.

He hooked the lines around the whip socket just in case he needed both hands. The nearest warrior was now so close Jeff could make out the smears of yellow warpaint on the dark chest, and the large yellow circles painted around the eyes giving the distorted face a crazy, grinning look.

With great strides the redskin bounded forward. The tomahawk began to twirl, faster and faster. Flash! The weapon whipped through the air. Jeff flopped to the seat as the weapon flashed by inches above his head.

The near oxen bellowed, the tomahawk ground into its flank, hanging there a full thirty seconds before it dropped to the earth. Blood spurted from the gaping wound and Jeff saw the animal stagger.

"Oh, Lord, help me now!" Jeff pleaded. The wagon slowed, but the lumbering oxen kept its feet and half dragged by the other managed to keep going.

The Indian closed up to within six feet of him. Jeff raised the whip and lashed at the hideous face. The knotted tip flicked the right cheek. The Indian dropped back; made a dash again. Jeff swung again. The Indian dodged. With a shriek he hurdled to the tailboard. Using the heavy butt end of the whip Jeff smashed at the shaven head, just where the scalp lock was knotted. The Indian, stunned by the blow, toppled off, regained his feet and charged again.

This time he hooked a long red hand around the rope that held the canvas, and before Jeff could ward him off the redskin was aboard. A sickening sweet odor scented the air from the perspiring Indian. Jeff slashed with the whip, but the redskin was waiting for the move and with a fury of hate tore it loose, flinging it off the wagon. Then screaming wildly, he lunged forward.

Jeff felt the wet, naked shoulder plunge into the pit of his stomach sending his breath out with a snort. Long fingers, hard as iron, curled toward his throat. Jeff flopped on his back, the Indian on top. With a sudden effort Jeff kicked. The Indian grunted and swung a fist at Jeff's nose. Blood rushed from the blow and before Jeff could twist away the Indian was upon him. The fingers found their mark, squeezing and twisting cruelly.

Time after time Jeff chopped blows at the circled eyes. Desperate for breath he saw blood run from a cut in the redman's cheek, but still the strangle hold tightened. Fifty feet away Jeff saw the other two redskins tearing toward the wagon with tomahawks drawn.

Jeff struggled until his feet were doubled under the Mohawk's stomach. With all the power he could muster he kicked. The hold around his neck loosened momentarily.

His legs thrashed, finding their mark. The Indian tumbled to one side. Jeff gasped for breath, the air cut ribbons in his burning throat.

"Now!" Jeff felt strength return as he swung his fist into the warrior's face. A shot rang out. Jeff moaned. "The other redskins!"

But to his amazement he saw the other two stop in their tracks. Suddenly they flashed away into the woods. The one on the wagon wiggled toward Jeff again.

Jeff waited until the last moment. When the hate-maddened face came close he lunged with a solid blow to the high cheek bone.

Another shot, Jeff twisted his aching neck and saw the yellow-logged stockade only fifty feet away. A group of armed men were atop the blockhouse. Relief flooded him. The shots had come from there!

A surge of thanksgiving welled in Jeff. Through blood-smeared eyes he saw one of the men raise his gun and fire toward the woods. He saw the great log gate opening as the oxen, spent and exhausted, dragged the wagon through. He heard the shouts of men and felt their hands, rough and yet gentle lower him to the ground. He saw them take the unconscious redskin and bind the slender arms and legs with rawhide.

He felt water forced between his lips, and his neck, swollen and red, throbbed with pain. Someone washed his face with soothing warm water.

Everything seemed painful, but Jeff didn't care. His heart was joyful; the Lord had heard his prayer. He was safe and there was the wagon, intact, even though it did appear to be bouncing up and down even yet, crawling with wild red-faced men.

Slowly the semi-conscious dream came to an end. Jeff stared into the ruddy, weather-beaten face of a snowy whiskered man bending over him. "I guess I made it," his words had a strange, faraway sound.

"Ya did just that, but another minute and you'd be minus that black hair of yours. We drove them other two off with a few shots. It's a pity we didn't puncture their red hides."

Jeff tried to sit up, but again he seemed to be jouncing along on the wagon in a crazy nightmare, so he lay back and felt the rain pelt his face with sweet cool drops of comfort.

Suddenly he remembered. Still gasping for breath he forced the words from his aching throat, "Send help! Carl Ives and the Watsons are back at the brook. Send help!"

Vaguely he saw the circle of faces draw back. He heard the old man's booming voice ordering a party to retrace the wagon tracks and see if they could find Carl and the Watsons. But that was all he remembered. His eyes and ears just wouldn't operate any longer.

He didn't hear Captain Snow's bellowing voice say, "That boy is done in. Look at them finger prints on his neck, and that gash over his eye. He had a time of it, I tell you. Get him under shelter and put dry clothes on him. Patch that cut on his forehead. With a good night's sleep he'll be all right. A big, strong lad like him don't stay broken in fer long."

7

"He's A Traitor!"

WHEN JEFF awoke from restless sleep in midafternoon the rain had stopped; and the sun was out, already at work drying the countless puddles in the Killypox stockade.

He ran his fingers along his stiff neck. How it did ache! Not only his neck, but also his shoulders, arms and legs. He ached all over for that matter, a dull tired feeling that made him just want to lie quiet like forever.

Opening his eyes, Jeff saw a robust, stout woman sitting by his side. She shook a leafy maple branch over his head and smiled, "The flies are a mite bad. Blacksmith's shop draws them over yonder, so I figured with nothing else to do I'd shoo them away awhile."

Jeff opened his lips to tell his thanks, but no words would come. "You just lie still. Don't bother yerself about nuthin'. Old Sadie Terwilliger will care fer ya," the woman purred softly.

He watched her leave the tiny room, but she returned a moment later with a wooden bowl of steaming broth. "Here, sip this up. It'll sooth that inside of yours and perk ya up." Jeff tried to smile while the woman laddled spoonful after spoonful down his searing throat.

"I looked ya all over and ya don't appear busted up much. Just that gash on yer head which ain't nuthin', and those finger marks around yer neck. 'Pears like the redskin

aimed to twist that curly black scalp of yours plumb off by
the looks of things."

Jeff heard his reply, hoarse and only a whisper, "He
sure tried." Then the question that plagued him was out, "Did
the men bring in Carl Ives and the Watson family?"

The old woman let her face show the answer. The
tired, wrinkled lines seemed to multiply around her thick lips,
"No, they ain't found nuthin' yet. The first party come in
hours ago and said not a track was seen. They went out agin,
but ain't back yet."

Struggling against the pain, Jeff raised himself to a
sitting position. "I'd better go see the Captain and tell him
I'm going out. I know just where they'll be."

He swung his legs over the cot and stood up, but only
for a second. His wobbly legs wouldn't hold.

"Pears like you ain't goin' no place. Here, sit in the
doorway on this bench. That warm sun will do ya a heap
of good."

Powerless to do anything else, Jeff sat looking over the
largest stockade he had ever seen. Sheds lined the inside walls
where at least fifty cows were tied, along with horses, goats and
a few donkeys. A log sty was filled with grunting pigs
and another housed sheep.

Women and children swarmed all over the place. A
game of tag was in full swing among the younger boys and
girls. Some of the women chatted, while others busied themselves churning butter, sewing, pounding corn or cooking over
the fire pits.

Above, on the lookout ramps, he could see frontiers-
men stationed, muskets ready. The woman answered the
questioning in his mind. "I guess it seems like a heap of
folks to you. There's a reason. These red raiders have been
plaguing the woods fer the last two weeks. Most every cabin
within three miles is burnt out. There's been killing and
there's been a heap of folks carried away captive. Most

everybody is stayin' here now. It's thicker with people than a bean plant is with beetles, but it's safe."

A crowd of young people caught Jeff's eye. He wondered at what was drawing their interest until he saw the Mohawk tied up against a pole, his red face still smeared with clay, but now mixed with a generous amount of blood. *I wonder how much of that is mine,* Jeff thought.

The Watson wagon stood just inside the door where he had left it. The two oxen were unyoked and the injured one was lying down while a man covered the wound with grease to keep the flies away.

"I'm the caretaker of the sick," the woman smiled. "This here place you was in is what I call my hospital. 'Tain't large, but that mattress you was on is filled with wild Canadian goose. feathers and I always say there's nuthin' better'n a good comfortable sleep to help the sick."

To the right of the tiny one-roomed log hospital stood a bark-roofed longhouse with three chimneys rising above the roof. Jeff knew this to be the place where the women and children stayed during a raid.

Beyond that place stood several smaller cabins where the regular residents of the fort lived. Directly across from the main blockhouse stood a double-doored building. Black smoke curled from the chimney and a noisy clanging made him wonder.

Again the woman saw the question in his face. "That's the blacksmith shop. Jedson Loon runs it."

"Miss Terwilliger—" Jeff began, but the woman stopped him.

"Not Miss, young feller, I'm Mrs. My man was out in the hayfield last June. I was choppin' kindlin' fer the fire when I heard his shot. I looked up and seen a redskin drop in his tracks by the edge of the woods. Then my man comes tearing towards me, but he never did git thar. A arrow smacked him 'tween the shoulders and he tumbled head-

long. That's the last I ever seen of him. I dodged behind
the house, knowin' there was nuthin' I could do, and crawled
up on our horse and came to Killypox. The redskins was
afoot so's they didn't git me. Next day some of the fellers
here went over and buried my man. That's why I'm Mrs.," the
woman's face showed her everlasting sorrow.

Jeff forgot his question and stared moodily at the pall
of smoke from the blacksmith shop. Captain Snow, atop the
blockhouse, bellowed, "Here comes the search party, but they
be alone."

The gate opened and the men filed in dejectedly. Jeff
walked painfully to meet them. One little runt of a man, with
long, dirty yellow hair matted over his narrow brow, said to
Captain Snow, "We followed that stream fer three miles to
the north and all the way to the river to the south and didn't
see nuthin! Maybe that kid was lying when he said there
was them others with him. I can't picture Carl Ives gettin'
caught by redskins."

"No, Lumberkin, the kid's telling the truth. I looked
over the wagon and found Watson's name in a Bible. Besides,
Carl Ives' pack sack was on top. His initials are burned in
the leather."

"Well, anyway, they ain't out there as we could find,"
Lumberkin insisted.

Captain Snow noticed Jeff, "Hello, thought you'd still
be takin' it easy. How you feelin'?"

"I ache all over a little, but it's not so bad," Jeff
paused. Then he said, "Captain, I'm going out for them."

The white whiskers popped with the brisk answer,
"I'm Captain here. You'll not move from this place." The
man walked away leaving Jeff alone.

Mournfully Jeff returned to the bench at the hospital
door only to find the gigantic form of Sadie Terwilliger there
holding a month old baby. "I'm sorry yer folks ain't found,
but keep hopin', maybe they'll turn up. Say, I guess you'll

have to find somewhere else to stay. This here baby's Mom is layin' on the feather mattress. She's took awful sick with the back complaint. Try the blacksmith shop. Most folks don't like to sleep there cause of the smell and flies, but Jedson Loon stands it and a young feller like you should be able to last out a night."

Later Jedson Loon nodded to Jeff, but finished pounding a horse shoe into shape before he lowered the hammer. "You feelin' better?" he asked.

"Some. Mrs. Terwilliger sent me over. The hospital cot's taken and anyway, I'm not so bad off I need the feather bed. I was wondering if I could put up here for the night."

Jed Loon grinned, "If you can stand the smell it suits me. I don't mind it, but some does."

The shop held the peculiar odor of burned hoofs and scorched hair. The smoke from the hand-pumped bellows clung to the raftered ceiling in a smudgy fog. Hundreds of flies hummed about the place. The white horse haltered near the door stomped his feet, quivered his skin, and flisked his tail constantly to drive the nipping pests away.

Jeff walked to the wagon, found his blankets, and laid them on the floor behind a junk heap of horse shoes and leather. Two red-coated deer mice scampered away when he moved a plank to make room for the bed. *What with the flies and mice I'll not be lacking for company, I guess,* he thought.

"If you want to be useful, you'll tackle that heap of old horse shoes and divide them up according to size. I ain't had time fer a month to do nuthin' but shoe horses and repair muskets. If I was takin' money fer my labor I'd be rich," the smith said, lifting up the white horse's left forefoot to fit the metal.

Jeff complied with the suggestion, anxious to rid his mind of his troubled worry about the missing travelers. At six, a cowbell clanged and he walked with Jed Loon to the longhouse for supper. Piping hot corn meal bread and venison stew were dished out in generous helpings. Every mouthful made his throat sting, but his hunger urged him to empty the plate.

At dusk the smith took his position on the ramp for guard duty. Jeff curled up on the blanket amid the heavy smells. He heard the noise of the others making ready for the night, wondering at the calmness with which they accepted the disappearance of his friends.

"I suppose you get used to sorrow and calamity after a while," he told himself.

Prayer filled his mind for the next half hour. Prayer, not only for the Watsons and Carl Ives, but also for his father, mother and sister. Albany seemed a faraway place. He wondered idly if he would ever walk the city streets again, or see and smell the bread dough laid in the ovens by his mother, or taste the maple sugar cookies, fresh and sweet. He remembered the happy years before the war when his father drove around the city with bread and cake for sale.

A shout interrupted his thoughts, "Somebody's coming up the river!" Captain Snow boomed from the blockhouse.

"Who's there?" rang out another voice.

"Carl Ives and party!" Jeff heard the distant reply with a rush of joy.

Leaping to his feet, despite a twinge of pain, he hastened to the gate. He heard it swing open and then the shuffle of footsteps told him Carl and the Watsons were coming in.

The first words came from Mr. Watson, "Did Jeff get the wagon through? Is he all right?"

"A young feller brung in a wagon and he also brung in a redskin he'd captured," Captain Snow answered.

"Here I am," Jeff said in the darkness. He felt Carl's arm circle his neck affectionately.

They gathered in the blockhouse where several candles were lighted after the door was closed to keep in the telltale rays. Jeff sat on one side while the Watsons and Carl ate their first food since early morning.

Maud sat near him and said, "Jeff, we thought surely you were dead. After we hid in a clump of bushes overhanging the stream we saw three Mohawks chasing you. Then we heard shots, two of them close together, and then silence. It was terrible out there wondering what happened."

"Those two shots were fired at me, but the redskin's aim was 'way off. But what happened to you? Two searching parties went out and returned with no signs of your trail."

"Well, we waited for an hour after the shots and then moved downstream, still walking in that icy water, until we came to the river. Carl led us along the bank for about a mile and then we stayed in a blackberry thicket the rest of the day. Poor little Pam cried most of the time, she was so hungry. I expected to see the Indians come any minute."

"I can tell you it wasn't pleasant just waiting here, thinking you were taken captive, or maybe even scalped," Jeff shuddered.

While Jeff had been talking to Maud, Captain Snow told about his wild ride. Carl called, "Jeff, that was some experience you had. That's the kind of courage that'll someday make this wilderness safe for the settlers."

Inwardly Jeff felt pride well up, but remembering his terrifying fright while the chase was raging, shame replaced his pride and he was glad for the dim candle light that hid his flushing face.

When Jeff left his bed in the blacksmith shop for breakfast the next morning his neck still gave him trouble, but it was some better.

He found that Maud had saved a place for him at the long table. Captain Snow and Lumberkin the scout sat nearby. The conversation drifted, as most conversations did in the 1770's and 80's, to the raging war between the settlers and the English.

Captain Snow's rollicking booming voice filled the entire building. He brought his fist down so hard on the table the wooden bowls danced. "Never!" he shouted. "Never will I pay another cent in taxes to them English. Them fellers who dressed up like Indians in Boston in 1773 and tossed three hundred and fifty chests of tea into the bay had the right idea," his eyes glowed with the thought, "*Oh, how I wish I had been with them.*"

"I'll be so glad when we're at peace again," Mrs. Watson sighed wistfully, looking at Pam.

Lumberkin told her, "Mrs. Watson, don't you worry none. That cabin yer husband built last year is still standin'. I see it the other day when I was up there."

Mr. Watson looked surprised, "Well, I never expected to hear that. I thought everything was burned out."

"Well, your land lies off the traveled path somewhat and you're hemmed in by mountains except on the south side. Them English and Indians never thought to look up there, I figure."

"Do you suppose it would be safe to go up there now?" Mr. Watson asked. "The planting season's getting late and I want to put in crops on that acreage I cleared last year."

"I wouldn't chance taking the women folk up there. There hasn't been two days the last month that Indians ain't been in this section. The only safe place is right here in the fort. With that cannon we have atop the blockhouse they're scared to death to attack us," Captain Snow pointed out.

"If you want ter git a crop this year, you'd better git up thar and work," Lumberkin muttered over a bowl of gruel.

"Take Jeff along with you, and when I get back from scouting the English forces up toward Niagara Falls I'll come give you a hand," Carl suggested.

Jeff spoke, "I'd like to, but I must push on to Fort Stanwix."

"Why?" Captain Snow asked.

"Well, sir, I've come from Albany on a mission. You see, sir, my father left last spring and promised to return in the fall, but up to now not a single word has been heard from him."

Jeff noticed Carl Ives stiffen and give his entire attention to buttering a piece of corn pone.

Captain Snow leaned forward and stared at Jeff, "Say, what did you say your name was?"

"Jefferson Lockwood."

"And what was yer father's name?"

"Samuel Lockwood."

The answer charged the group. Lumberkin half rose to his feet, an angry scowl fleeting his face. Captain Snow shoved his plate away and snorted in open disgust. Even Carl Ives acted strange.

"You'll not be needin' to go further to git word of him," Lumberkin whined sarcastically.

Hope flooded Jeff, but hope faded and failed a moment later when Captain Snow pushed back his bench and rose to his feet. His eyes blazed angrily, and the chin whiskers jutted and popped as he rasped in disgust, "Yer father was here with us last year. He ain't now, though. Yer father turned out to be a traitor to his country. He's as bad as Benedict Arnold hisself. Yer father went over to the enemy."

E

8

"Any Fish?"

LIKE CRACKING, jagged lightning zipping over the Mohawk Valley during a thunder storm, the words, "Your father is a traitor!" echoed through Jeff's unbelieving mind.

Dumbly, he stared at Captain Snow. The man's face showed only scorn. Lumberkin smirked as though he were pleased with Jeff's discomfort. Carl Ives looked helplessly on as he said, "Jeff, I'm sorry. I had heard about your father."

"But, Carl, why didn't you tell me? Why didn't you tell me?"

"I didn't say anything because I wasn't sure, Jeff. I'm still not sure for that matter."

Jeff felt a glimmer of hope emerging from his despair, but Lumberkin sounded a quick end to that ray of encouragement.

"You may not be dead certain about Lockwood's desertion, Ives, but I am. That man drifted in here last year and I knew him from the first; tall, dark-haired fellow like his son. He worked with us to build this fort and went out lots of times on forays. He always kept askin' about the loyalty of the settlers in this section. Well, there was one feller, Dunken Knore by name, we always figured was for the English, secret like. We told Lockwood, and before long he was livin' at that Tory's house.

"Then one day we had a terrible raid. We blasted

62

the cannon to call everyone to the fort fer safety, but Lockwood and Knore didn't come. As soon as things quieted down I took off to Knore's place and seen right away where they'd cleared out. Well, curious to see what happened to Lockwood, I trailed the raiders. Sure enough, I came upon them at Canada Creek, and who was among them, but Lockwood, just as free and easy being with the enemy as you like. I drew a bead on that traitor's head and almost pulled the trigger, but knew right well I'd be a goner if I was to do it, so I held fire, figuring my life was worth more than that skunk's."

When Lumberkin concluded his story Captain Snow nodded in agreement, "He's speakin' the truth. That man was good fer nuthin'."

"I'm still not sure," Carl insisted.

"Nor am I," Mr. Watson broke in, "I'm not at all sure. True, it was an odd succession of events, but to condemn a man before he can speak for himself is unfair."

"Even if Samuel Lockwood is guilty of treason, I'll string along with Jeff," Carl spoke up. "He brought in that wagon and risked his skin in doing it. Besides, this same boy was hoodwinked by a man named Kittle awhile back. In fact, he was taken prisoner by Kittle and Haynes and finally escaped. Now I ask you, would a young fellow be likely to be taken prisoner by the enemy if he were their friends? Not likely, I'd say."

Lumberkin wheezed, "Ives, you're wrong. I always say, like father, like son; and I tell ya now, I don't trust this boy fer a musket ball."

Captain Snow bellowed as he always did, his voice carrying to where the other prisoners were eating, "Jefferson Lockwood, my advice to you is to plan on leavin' Killypox just as soon as you can. You're not welcome here. These people have suffered enough without the son of a traitor dwellin' with them. Innocent or guilty, whatever you may be, your hide will be safer far way."

"Aren't you being unfair, Captain Snow?" Mr. Watson asked quietly. "You can't judge a boy without the slightest evidence!"

"I have these people to consider," Captain Snow waved toward the settlers who were showing their displeasure of what they had heard. "Men, women and children have been killed, and until Samuel Lockwood has been proven innocent we want none of his son!" Jeff saw many of the people nod in agreement.

He rose to his feet and walked out into the morning sun. Carl and Mr. Watson followed. Turning to face his friends, he said, "I'll leave this morning! I'll go into the English lines. I'll hunt every inch of the country until I prove my father innocent of these false charges!"

"Wait, Jeff," Carl pleaded. "Wait! You'd never find your father that way. The woods are filled with prowlers and they'd have your scalp in no time."

"Look, Jeff," Mr. Watson said, laying a restraining hand on the boy's·jacket sleeve. "My cabin is ten miles north of here. There's heaps of work to be done and I need help. Come with me. I'm leaving this morning. Come and help me plant the crops."

"Do it, Jeff. Mr. Watson's right. I'm to leave tomorrow to scout the English. I'll keep my eyes peeled for your Dad. But don't rush off and ruin everything," Carl pleaded.

The men were right; Jeff knew it, and finally answered reluctantly, "All right, I'll go with you, Mr. Watson, but at the first opportunity I'm leaving to get this mess straightened out. I couldn't stand it if I didn't. I know my father is as loyal as George Washington. And when we find the answer Captain Snow will be the first to hear of it. I'll tell him myself."

"Let's pack up immediately and head for my place," Mr. Watson suggested.

Mrs. Watson and Maud prepared enough foodstuffs for two weeks while the men rolled blankets, axes, shovels, hoes, shot and ammunition for hunting. Within an hour they were ready.

Into the woods they went; the forest, damp from the recent rains, blazed with wild flowers. Violets, buttercups and spring beauties scented the air. "I thought to bring the oxen but Carl said it was too big a risk. That means we'll have to do the planting by hand," Mr. Watson said.

"I'm glad there's work to be done. It'll keep my mind from fretting," Jeff told the missionary.

At noon they rested beside a moss-banked spring and ate in silence. When the last scrap was cleaned up Mr. Watson leaned back against a sycamore tree, "Jeff, that was a hard blow you had this morning."

"It's all of that. Why it's got me so down-hearted I could almost burst."

"I guess I'd feel about the same way," Mr. Watson agreed. "Yet there's something to remember. Did you ever see those eagle wings Carl Ives has burned on his moccasins?"

"Yes, I noticed them."

"Well, there's a reason for that. Carl told me about it. He said that often he got so discouraged that he just stared at the ground. Then one day he was reading his Bible and came across a verse in Isaiah that meant a great deal to him. Perhaps you've read it yourself. It goes, 'They that wait upon the Lord shall renew their strength; they shall mount up with wings as eagles; they shall run, and not be weary; and they shall walk, and not faint.'

"So Carl decided to burn those eagle wings in his moccasins as a constant reminder. When discouragement tugged and got him looking down he would see the wings and recall the verse. That's not a bad idea, Jeff."

"What does it mean to wait upon the Lord, Mr. Watson"?

"Jeff, first of all it means prayer; then after that it means the patience to wait until the Lord answers that prayer."

"Pray and wait." Jeff, in his desperation, clung to these words. Even years later, when he recalled the trying times of bygone wilderness days, those same words still echoed. No, more than echoed; they became the pattern and guide for his entire life.

"Well, Jeff, we'd best move on," Mr. Watson said a half hour later, rising to his feet and leading the way. "I still have doubts of finding the cabin intact."

"But Lumberkin said he saw it not long ago."

"I know, but there have been several raids since then."

They trudged on through the forest until Mr. Watson stopped atop a rise. "Well, now, I was wrong. Look there!"

The forest broke into a level bottom land clearing, fringed on the south side by a deep, fast moving stream. To the west a wooded mountain formed a natural barrier. Facing the stream, but several hundred yards from it, Jeff saw the cabin, small and still yellowish, for the logs had not yet taken on the weather-beaten brown color of older cabins.

The cleared land was black in the afternoon sun, promising rich crops for the family. Mr. Watson nodded toward the fields, "Years ago that used to be under water. There was an old beaver pond here then, and the soil is about as good as you could find. Only a few small trees had taken root, so I had an easy time cleaning it off."

They hurried down into the vale. Jeff supposed he had never seen a likelier spot for a home. Behind the cabin, rising but a few feet away, was a massive shale cliff at least fifty feet high. Scrub pine and heavy vines clung to the almost perpendicular slope.

"I built the cabin there so the mist hanging over the stream would be as distant as possible. Besides the bluff in back will keep the north wind from swishing through the cracks when winter comes."

"Are there any fish down there?" Jeff pointed to a deep hole.

"Come on. We need some fresh meat for supper. Let's see what we can catch," Mr. Watson suggested.

Jeff cut two long slender hickery poles, while Mr. Watson found worms under the stones along the bank. Within ten minutes they were easing up to a deep pool. Jeff cast near a tremendous boulder in midstream. Almost at once the line shot away. A brook trout scurried wildly to free the hook, but Jeff worked the fish into shore and then flipped him on the grassy bank.

"I guess that proves we can have a fresh fish dinner when we want it," Mr. Watson laughed. A moment later the missionary's rod bent waterward as a lunker of a fish took the worm. With a dash the trout frisked under an overhanging tree. The line tangled and the trout went free. "We'll have to get him some day. He was a whopper!" Mr. Watson groaned, tying on a new hook.

Before a half hour passed they had four fish, each about ten inches long, and just right for the frying pan. Before they ate Mr. Watson and Jeff kneeled in front of the cabin in thanksgiving.

Jeff's everlasting burden seemed lighter when the man finished. The folks at the stockade were remembered, as were Jeff's folks back home, but the most comforting part about the prayer was Mr. Watson's asking the Lord to watch over Jeff's father. The certainty of the answer to the request flooded him. Somehow, someday, somewhere, the missing man would be discovered.

9

"The Heron Was Afraid"

CRAMMED DAYS, full of hard, back-breaking work followed. The seeds were dropped in the long rows Jeff trenched with a hoe. It would have been much easier with the oxen, yet the work wasn't unpleasant and the dip each evening in the cold brook was a stimulating treat.

On Saturday Mr. Watson announced, "Jeff, I'm going in to Killypox first thing in the morning. Captain Snow asked me to take tomorrow's preaching service and I don't want to miss the opportunity to help all I can. I'll probably stay at least a week. How would you like to come with me?"

"No, I think not. It would be the best part of good judgment to avoid a run in with Captain Snow about my father. I'll stay here. I'd like to clear those bushes from the stream so that we can have a nice place to draw water.

"If the reports are comforting I think I'll bring the family back when I come," Mr. Watson said, "I miss them more than I can tell. I'll also bring the wagon and we can fit the windows and hang the door."

Sunup found Jeff alone, Mr. Watson having left long before the spring beauties along the brook curled open in the morning light. A strange stillness shrouded the homestead, and it puzzled him for a while until he remembered it was actually the first time he had been that far away from a human being. It gave him a thrill of freedom and when he took the axe to clear the brush from the stream bank he tackled it with a pleasant enthusiasm.

By noon the task was completed and Jeff flopped on a flat rock watching the swirling water bubble toward the Mohawk River to the south. "The river means the end of the brook in that direction but what lies upstream? I think I'll go exploring and find out," Jeff decided.

The stream curled, snake-like fashion, toward a broken hump-backed stretch of mountains. They formed an almost impossible barrier for invading raiders from that direction. The water way narrowed as it cut through a steep rock-sided gorge.

"Looks like this is the end of my exploration, I could never wade through." Jeff watched the swirling, tumbling white foam lick the slippery boulder he squatted on. Moss and lichens clung to the surface of the spray dampened rocks and made the footing treacherous. The sun, except at midday, never sent its drying rays into the cavern, and the coolness was almost uncomfortable.

As Jeff studied the glen he felt dwarfed beside the perpendicular walls towering up at least sixty feet. "Say, that looks like a ridge up there. I just wonder if I could make it." Moving with caution, Jeff worked along the stream until he found a section of cliff pocked with jagged crevices. Inch by inch, and foot by foot, he ascended until he gained the ridge that ran parallel with the stream and twenty feet above it.

The boiling water sent a haze of spray vapor even that high. *This place seems almost enchanted,* he thought.

The ledge broadened to a barren rock-topped plateau and from here Jeff could see over a vast virgin wilderness. He saw Killypox, just a light brown speck in the forest, with a pall of smoke from the fires, the silver ribbon of the Mohawk River running near by.

The plateau was about a half acre in extent. A black

spot against the lighter gray of the stone caught his attention. Upon investigating, he gasped, "Why, this is the remainder of a fire. And there's another, and another!" Suddenly it occurred to Jeff that the spots were arranged in a distinct pattern, "Indians! That's it! They use this place for a signaling station."

Alarmed with this knowledge he tried to find the Watson cabin, but much to his relief, not a single log showed, nor did the clearing. "Well I must be ten miles from home, anyway, so maybe it's not as bad as I figured."

With that consolation he backtracked toward the stream.

At dusk Jeff walked into the cabin, dead tired and hungry, but satisfied with the knowledge of the country he had gained. Every day, for the next three, he traveled about the tiny wilderness home. He constantly practiced identifying animal tracks and bird calls. He jotted down any that were uncertain, planning to question Carl at their next meeting. He found himself moving through the woods with a greater degree of quietness and thrilled when he almost stepped on a deer one afternoon.

"That means I moved so quietly she couldn't hear me. I guess that's a pretty good sign."

On Friday he loitered about the home, pulling weeds and hoeing the corn which already poked its green shoots through the dark soil. He also built a bench around the sturdy trunk of a maple near the doorway of the cabin. When he finished he took his Bible from his pack and read the entire Book of John before evening's fading light caused him to close the wonderful pages. Since his acquaintance with Carl and Mr. Watson, he found the Christian life a great deal more interesting than he had ever imagined it could be.

He climbed up the steep slope behind the cabin midmorning the following day. The stones he loosened as he went tumbled down to bounce off the heavy bark roof.

Halfway up the bluff he stumbled upon a small opening, so small he just could wiggle through into what appeared to be a cave. In the vague light he looked about a rock-walled room about twenty feet square and six feet high, with a tunnel leading downward.

The discovery enchanted Jeff. "I'll get a dry pine torch and light it so I can explore that tunnel." The sides were lined with a rather soft, dry, powdery stone that enabled him to scratch his initials in several places.

For thirty feet the tunnel led down until it came to another vault, not as large as the top room, but just as tinder dry and high. Quite suddenly he had an idea. "Say, I do believe this room is lower than the cabin. If I could dig a tunnel through from the floor above, it would make just about the most wonderful hiding place you could find."

He retraced his steps and hurried down the slope to the cabin. Taking the axe he chopped a stout oak sapling and chipped one end until he had a sharp point. This he hardened by thrusting it into the fire until blackened.

"Now, let's see. I'll try here first." He plunged the point into the ground and pounded the blunt end with the axe. It sank three feet and then jammed against a rock and would go no further.

Again he tried in the opposite end of the cabin. The point drove steadily to the three foot mark and then stopped again. Jeff stepped back and swung the axe with all his strength hitting the oak stake square. With unexpected suddenness the pole shot down. "I must have broken through" Jeff thought, as he dashed from the cabin, up the slope, to the cave mouth above. Using the torch which he had left in such a position as to keep burning, he worked down the tunnel and right in the dead center of the sunken vault he saw the oak stake extending down.

Fired with his plan for the safety tunnel he tore into the task. He worked from the top, digging out the soft soil until the shovel hit the harder, powdery stone. Then the going went slower, for Jeff had to practically chop away every inch.

It was late when he cut through the eighteen inch layer of soft sandstone. He fashioned a ladder to fit the hole and enable him to crawl down. The accomplishment gave him a surge of happiness he hadn't experienced ever before, and as he curled up on the upper cave room for the night it was with a glow of satisfaction that ended in thanksgiving to the Lord for the joys of the wilderness life.

All day Sunday Jeff rested in a shaded glen near the brook. He watched a *towhee chewink* feed its nest full of babies. Both the mother and father bird helped bring bugs. Finally, the hungry mouths closed and the youngsters went to sleep.

A rich brown coated muskrat wobbled along the bank, followed by three little baretailed kits. They came within three feet of Jeff's moccasins, and in that moment he realized one of the greatest secrets of studying wild life — that of lying motionless until the animals and birds were unaware of one's presence. Jeff tried it in different places that day, and each time he saw something new and interesting. In an oak grove he spotted nine squirrels at one time. *Why, I never suspected there were so many*, he thought as a light gray, half-grown jerky tail whisked up a tree. He returned to the cove in the late afternoon with his Bible. He read for an hour then stretched out for a nap. Almost at once he saw a shadow fall near by. A huge blue-gray bird, with lengthy, slender red legs dropped on the edge of the stream. Jeff recognized it as a great blue heron. Often he had seen them from a distance, but never so close as now. Why, he could even see the two black tuffs of feathers jutting straight back from the bird's white face. He watched the long bill dart into a weeded bed in shallow water. A tiny frog was the victim and the bird gobbled it down, and again stood perfectly still for another tasty frog to blunder into range.

On the opposite bank Jeff saw the shadowy form of a fox emerge from a clump of wild rice. The heron lifted itself on heavy wings at the enemy's appearance and the fox saw Jeff and it too fled.

"Well," Jeff laughed, "it looks as though everything in the woods has to fight for life. The frog fell to the heron, the heron was afraid of the fox, the fox is afraid of me, and I have to watch out for Indians."

On Monday afternoon Jeff was squatted in the bean patch, pulling weeds, when he heard the distant sound of someone approaching. He figured it was the Watsons, but rather than risk a trap, he slipped into the woods until he saw the black oxen poke their flat blunt muzzles into the clearing.

10

"Look, A Bear"

WHEN JEFF saw the canvas wagon roll into view he suddenly realized how lonely he had been since Mr. Watson left. With a rush of love for the missionary family, he ran toward them, waving his hands in enthusiastic greeting. He took Pam from Mrs. Watson. She gurgled contentedly when Jeff poked a grimy finger into her plump little middle. "'Seems like she almost remembers me," he grinned.

Mrs. Watson and Maud stared at their new wilderness home. Mr. Watson waited to one side, watching the expression on their faces. It was Maud who burst out, "Why, Daddy, it's wonderful! It's the prettiest place I ever saw. And the garden! Look, the seeds are up already. And the cabin, why it's just wonderful! Oh, I'm going to love it here."

Mrs. Watson added softly, "It is lovely. I feel at home already."

"I'm glad you both like it. How about that, Jeff?"

"I'm sure glad they do, and I guess Pam here thinks it's a pretty nice place. See her smiling."

"Say, Jeff, take a look behind the wagon. There's a present there for the family." Jeff puzzled for a moment, but when he stepped to one side he caught view of a soft-eyed brown cow.

"Wow, isn't she a beauty!"

"She's more than that. She means fresh milk, butter and cheese, not to mention the calf she'll present us with in the fall."

"Jeff, Carl said to tell you he would be out in a few days for a visit."

"Did he mention any word of my father?"

"Only to say there was no news of him."

"Oh!" Jeff's voice revealed his discouragement.

Mr. Watson reminded, "Jeff, remember the eagle wings?"

Jeff forced a smile and turned his attention to the oxen and the new cow, while Mr. Watson led the family to the cabin. Suddenly Jeff remembered the cave, so he released the animals in the deep grass along the brook and ran to the cabin.

"Mr. Watson, I have a surprise for you. Look!" Jeff slid the flat stone he used to cover the hole in the ground, "This leads down to a big room-like vault, and another tunnel slants upward to another room halfway up the cliff. I found it when I saw a small cave opening up there." Jeff pointed to the spot and the family peered upwards.

"I can't see a thing that looks like a cave up there," Maud said, poking her head out the doorway.

"You can't from here, that's the best part of it. If raiders should swoop from the forest we could hide in the cave, cover the opening here in the cabin with this flat rock and see what was going on from up there without anyone knowing about it."

"Say," Mr. Watson exclaimed, "that's the best thing I ever heard of. But how did you dig through the rock?"

"It's soft sandstone, I think, and it wasn't as tough as you might expect. I finished it in one day." Armed with torches, Jeff led the way down the ladder.

Mr. Watson was entranced. "Jeff, this is the most wonderful thing I could imagine. Why, this place is dry enough for us to store our crops, and if a raid did come we could spend weeks in here without anyone knowing it."

Later, on a warm, windless day — the same day Jeff and Maud worked hoeing corn in their bare feet — Carl drifted in from Killypox.

"Hi there, farmers!" he hailed.

"Hello, Carl."

"Say, it looks dangerous around here. I do believe there's bears nearby."

Something in Carl's smile warned Jeff, but Maud innocently asked, "What makes you think so, Carl?"

"Well, young lady, look at all those bare tracks in that earth you and Jeff just hoed." Carl pointed to their footprints.

"Ohhh!" Maud groaned, but joined in the laughter.

"I'm sure glad to see you, Carl," Jeff said.

"I'm glad to see you, Jeff, but I can't stay as I first planned. Right this minute I'm on a mission to Oneida Lake to check the movements of an Indian village out there. Captain Snow wants an estimate on the number of warriors. Some talk is floating around about sending a force of militia up to try and scare them from that district."

Carl stayed only long enough to speak to the missionary and his wife. Then with a wave he strode into the woods. "Wow, I wish I were like him," Jeff breathed.

"He sure is wonderful, so tall and strong and yet so graceful as he walks," Maud added as they returned to hoeing.

When the corn was finished Jeff helped Mr. Watson fit the precious glass windows, a luxury few of the settlers enjoyed in that area. Most of the people used greased paper or deerskin, scraped thin, to allow a little gloomy light into the cabins. "Now," Mr. Watson said, "if raiders do come we have these frames fixed so they can be removed within a few minutes notice. I surely hope we won't see that day come, however."

The door, made of sturdy oak planks, was hung, and the cabin looked snug and tight from the inside. Three rooms were made, one tiny room for Maud, and another much larger for Mr and Mrs. Watson and the baby, while the third served as kitchen and dining room. Mr. Watson wanted Jeff to rig a bunk in this room, but he refused.

"After all, Mr. Watson, the cave is dry as a bone and I can easily sleep there." And sleep there he did, on a small cot and a mattress he made of sweet scented pine needles from the nearby woods. Even on hot nights he found the cool cave most comfortable.

A few weeks later Mr. Watson announced, "Jeff, I'm putting you in charge of my family while I go into Killypox to preach tomorrow."

"Sure," Jeff laughed, "but I reckon there'll be little to do. After all, no word of raiders has come to us for 'most a month."

After Mr. Watson hit the trail, Jeff suggested, "Maud, yesterday I saw a patch of wild blackcaps upstream aways. Let's go pick some. They're sweet as honey."

"Good, and I'll take Pam along to get some of this glorious sunshine."

"Be careful," warned Mrs. Watson. "Maud, you keep a watchful eye on Pam. You know how she likes to crawl."

"I will," Maud promised as they left. Jeff carried birch bark containers for the berries and also the musket Mr. Stiles had given him.

"Why the musket, Jeff?"

"Well, like Carl Ives said one time. 'If you go without being prepared there's always a chance you won't get back.' So this goes along just in case."

The patch was but a short quarter of a mile away from the cabin and the berries were as plentiful as scales on a fish, so before long they had two of the four containers brim full.

F

"Mother will probably want to make jam for next winter," Maud said, dropping a handful in one of the empty pails.

Pam played on a sunny ridge among a few dwarfed cedar trees. Both Jeff and Maud glanced her way every few moments. "If my mother, father and sister were out here with us, I'd think this was about the most perfect place in all the world," Jeff told Maud.

A gutteral snort from the knoll made both of them glance in that direction. Maud screamed in terror, "Jeff, look! A bear!" A ponderous black animal shuffled from behind a bush into full view, not more than ten feet from the baby.

At Maud's cry of alarm the bear swung to his hind feet and stared at them. Desperately Jeff looked to where the gun stood against a tree trunk twenty feet to his right. The bear grunted and dropped to all fours, sniffing toward Pam who showed an exasperating interest in the dangerous visitor. She gurgled and cooed in awe as the big bear watched her crawl towards him. Jeff eased his way toward the gun.

The bear, apparently bewildered by the pink cub that showed no fear, grunted and backed off as the baby crawled closer. Jeff dashed for the gun. He reached out for the barrel, but his trembling hand knocked it down. The bear heard the sound and reared again with a menacing growl. Immediately the huge beast dropped to its feet and loped toward Jeff with amazing swiftness. He grabbed the musket and hurriedly aimed. "One shot, and only one," the words were spoken aloud. The bear swung onward, now but fifteen feet away. Jeff's trigger finger pressed tight and a deafening roar crashed through the woods. The bear bellowed, stopped and lifted a huge padded forepaw in an attempt to wipe away the strange sting that hit his eye. Still growling and snorting the injured animal lumbered off a few feet and crumbled to the earth. Jeff, in the meantime, jammed another shot home, aimed and put the bear out of its misery.

Maud had caught up Pam, and still clinging to her cried out, "Oh, whatever would have happened if you had missed!"

"Worse than that. What would have happened if this old musket were back in the cabin. Wow, I shudder to think of it."

Pam wiggled to get down and when she touched the ground she crawled over and buried her head in the soft fur. "Just think, she doesn't know the danger she was in."

Jeff mopped his wet brow, "Well, I made up for her lack of knowledge, I can tell you!"

The berry picking venture ended abruptly. They returned to the cabin. Afterwards, Jeff and Maud skinned the bear and cut all the meat they could use for the table. Three days later they passed that way and found nothing but a pile of bones. The foxes, skunks and birds had also enjoyed the bear meat feast.

11

"Work Up Your Appetites!"

ON THE THIRD OF JULY Captain Snow sent the scout, Lumberkin, to tell the Watsons to come to the fort. Everyone was called in because of a large raiding party of English and Mohawks moving down from Canada. Carl Ives had been the news bearer and as soon as he had reported he was sent north again to determine the strength and the destination of the party.

Jeff, still not a welcome figure with anyone except Carl and the Watsons, stayed at the cabin. He moved everything, food and windows included, to the cave. For nine days he was alone; alone to wonder what he should do. As the time slid by slower than a grandfather turtle going up an ice-covered mountain, he felt he must not put off searching for his father much longer.

Yet, what could he do, or where could he go? Not a single clue had turned up on any of Carl's trips. There was nothing to do, only wait and ask the Lord to help.

On the twelfth of July the Watsons returned in the wagon, leading the cow behind.

"Carl Ives came back last night. The war party headed east toward Albany and there is much fear an attack might be made in that direction," Mr. Watson explained.

"Jeff, Carl is coming to see you tonight. He's going to spend a few days with us to rest up," Mrs. Watson added.

They replaced the windows and a few of the other things in the cabin, but left most of their belongings in the cave. Carl came in as they were seating themselves at the supper table.

"Join us, Carl," Mrs. Watson invited.

"It'll be good to eat at a table again. I've been chewing on parched corn and dried meat so long I forgot my manners," the scout said, wearily slumping on the bench.

Heads were bowed; Mr. Watson returned thanks, "Lord, we put our trust in Thee and thank Thee for this food. Bless it to our bodies and thus to Thy service. In Jesus' Name, Amen."

After the meal was finished Jeff showed Carl the cave. "This is the most remarkable thing I ever saw. It's almost fool proof unless someone knew about it. Don't tell a soul, white or red. Those secrets have a funny way of traveling."

The next morning, before the Watsons stirred, even before Dolly the cow got to her feet in the shed built for her, Carl and Jeff worked their way along the stream with their fishing lines. Slender hickory saplings served as poles.

"There's a deep hole upstream a mile. I never fished it, but it looks inviting," Jeff suggested.

They eased their way in pale dawn light, creeping cautiously to the rim of the quiet pool. The water was calm, dead still. A muskrat perched himself on a rock within six feet of the fishermen. Noiselessly the rich brown-coated animal slipped into the water, sending tiny ripples that grew and grew and grew until they seemed to bounce along the shore and disappear.

Jeff hooked into a big worm, dangled it above the water; lower, lower, it touched. A tremendous swirl, the pole bent against the lunging trout. The fish arched upward; out of the water and plunged deep again to sulk among the boulders.

"He's a whopper; Biggest I ever saw," Carl breathed.

Jeff didn't answer, the fish was running again. Up and

down the pool it swung, sometimes breaking the surface in splashing swirls, sometimes brooding and quiet at the bottom of the pool.

"His rushes aren't so strong any more. He's tiring," Jeff eased the fish near shore. A huge speckled beauty, it lay, weaving its fins as Jeff leaned over to grasp the gill flaps.

A swirl and away; the fish hadn't surrendered. Down, down, it went again, hovering near the bottom. Jeff tugged to stir him into motion. It worked, the trout shot for the surface, breaking water, sending a spray of drops into the sunlight.

Then it was over. The fish, exhausted and beaten, submitted to Jeff's fingers hooking in behind the gills to lift it free and clear of the water.

"The best trout I ever saw. He must go eight pounds if he goes an ounce," Carl decided.

"He feels that big," agreed Jeff, hefting his fish experimentally in his hand.

They tried for another, but the fight had made the other fish cautious, and they wouldn't touch the bait.

"Well, anyway, there's plenty for a feast," Jeff said.

"Say, Jeff, after breakfast let's you and I go out for a deer. I'm hungry for a juicy red steak."

"Fine, and there's some questions I want to ask you about tracking."

The fish sizzled on the black iron spider as Mrs. Watson seasoned it with salt and sweet butter.

Jeff and Carl sat in the doorway, sniffing the tempting aroma in anticipation. Pam crawled around, poking into everything she could reach. Maud boiled the coffee while Mr. Watson read aloud from his Bible the thirty-fifth chapter of Isaiah.

"It's odd how foolish some folks are — just living for gain. It's all right to make a fortune, I guess, but it's not for me. I'd rather have time to think, time to remember the Lord as the Master and Maker of all things. Now take that frying trout filling the air with goodness, he was put in that pool for us to catch and eat this morning," Carl Ives reflected.

"I agree," Mr. Watson nodded, "If a person takes time to seek the Lord and earnestly lives by God's Word, life is pleasant, for the sting of death is removed. Take that chapter I just read, the promises there are still in the future, and they're for us, seeing as how we love the Lord."

Jeff asked a question that had been plaguing his mind for some time, "I've been a Christian for about a year now, but there's lots of times I worry and there's lots of times I'm awful tempted into wrong doing, 'specially my thoughts. Will a time come when I'll be free from these tantalizing things?"

Mr. Watson answered, "Jeff, the Christian life is a battle. Satan is always trying to break you down. He'll keep doing that every day you live on earth, but there does come a time when these things fade into the background for the most part. Then your Christian life will be deeper."

Carl broke in, "I know how you feel, Jeff. It's worrisome, seeing how bad we are, but the Lord Jesus Christ saved us and it's on Him we can depend to keep us safe. I guess the best rule for a happy Christian life is to pray and read your Bible every single day. That's what cured me of a lot of off color habits and ideas. Still is curing me."

"Breakfast's ready!" Maud said, stopping any further talk, but Jeff was satisfied. If two men like Mr. Watson and Carl Ives advised prayer and Bible reading, it was for him also, for those two men were Christians through and through, and lived the lives to back up what they reckoned true.

"Now, Jeff, there's plenty of deer in those woods, but they can hide easy," Carl Ives said an hour later as they walked eastward along the brook. "The thing we have to do is track. Find where one drank from the stream and from there we move without a sound."

A sandy spot showed the pig-like tracks where three deer had watered. Carl whispered, "That's a doe with two half-grown fawns. You trail, I'll follow. Shoot the biggest of the fawns."

Jeff moved through the underbrush following easily the forked prints in the soft spongy earth. The deer led away toward higher ground, pausing now and then to nibble at green shoots.

A squirrel chattered from an oak, scolding at the white men who dared trespass. Jeff lost the trail in a small field, covered with huckleberry bushes. Carl took over and led the way slowly, testing the wind to see if the deer might have scented them.

"The wind is blowing from the deer to us. That's good, for their sense of smell is better than their sight. If the wind carried our scent to them we would have to give up," he whispered.

In the woods again Jeff took the trail. For a mile they traveled. A fern-filled glade appeared on their left, the tracks now faint in the drier ground, led into it. Carl laid a restraining hand on Jeff's shoulder and studied the glade.

Slowly he raised his hand and pointed to the rise on the far side. For five minutes Jeff peered. He saw nothing until a tiny motion caught his eye. Again he saw the movement, and slowly made out the head of a deep brown eyed doe. The flicking motion came from her ear as she twicked flies away.

To the deer's right another motion caught his eye. One of the fawns moved its head to lick its back. The other fawn wasn't to be seen, probably hidden behind its mother, Jeff reasoned.

Jeff raised his gun slowly. The barrel scraped against a branch. The deer leaped. Jeff aimed quickly at the fawn and fired. The deer bounded away unhurt. Carl's gun roared and the fawn fell, hit just behind the top of the right foreleg, a shot that reached the heart.

"Well, you did pretty good, Jeff. You managed to

trail them over some rough country, but you'll have to plan your motions more carefully. One mistake might mean hunger someday," Carl said as they skinned out the meat.

"Wow, they were hard to see!"

"Yes, they were. That's why you have to use your eyes. Being at home in the woods is a bigger thing than just hunting rabbits or squirrels. To really learn to know your way around, you have to be as curious as a six weeks old puppy. Investigate every trace, know what it is. If you don't know, then find out. Identify every bird call, every animal voice, from the squeak of a mouse to the howl of a bobcat. Learn the names of the trees and the flowers. Know every kind of snake and fish. If there's something that puzzles you, question somebody who does know. But be curious about everything."

Jeff rolled the deerhide into a bundle with the legs inside. Carl carried the rest over his shoulder.

The cabin door was swung open and Carl shouted, "Work up your appetites! We got one!"

Both Maud and Mrs. Watson hissed softly, "Shhhh, the baby's taking her morning nap."

Carl stopped dead short and tip-toed in, raising his moccasined feet and padding them silently on the hard earth floor. Jeff smiled inwardly to see that huge mountain of a man easing over to the crib, gazing so lovingly at the pink-cheeked Pam, sound asleep, with her little fist doubled over the bunny skin blanket. The gentle tenderness glowing in the scout's eyes made Jeff respect him all the more.

12

"A Scolding Blue Jay"

AUGUST with the burning hot days came upon them. The corn almost shot up over night. The beans and other crops prospered in the black soil.

"Most of the settlers have left the fort and returned to their farms," Mr. Watson told the family one Monday after he had been in to preach the day before. Crops were good all along the valley and there was even hope the Indian raids had come to an end. The reports from the other parts of the country drifted in; the Tories had taken several beatings, but so had the Continental Army.

"When the war is won, and the Indians and English are defeated, this country will be filled with settlers. Now there is no one within seven miles of us. Then we'll have neighbors on every side. I plan to put up a chapel as soon as I can, for where the towns and cities grow there must be a place for people to worship and a place to send forth the good news of eternal life in Christ Jesus," Mr. Watson told the family at dinner.

The missionary had brought home a pound of maple sugar which, divided equally, was a treat, for sweet things were scarce. Pam, with her tiny bit, crawled outside, where she nibbled amid contented chortles in the patch of sun near the door.

"Look at all those bees at the sugar Pam dropped," Maud exclaimed.

"They're planning to have some maple sugar honey I guess," commented Mrs. Watson.

"Honey!" exclaimed Jeff. "Where there's bees there must be honey!"

"What do you mean, Jeff?" Maud asked.

"I mean those bees must have a home and that home would be full of honey, and honey sure would go good on corn bread or on anything for that matter."

"How would you find it?" Mr. Watson questioned.

"Well, I never tried it, but I've heard the method described. You see which direction a bee takes and follow it as long as you can. Then you stop and hold out something sweet until one finds it. You trace him a few hundred feet, repeating the system, until you find the bee tree."

"Let's try," Maud suggested.

"They all go due west from here," Jeff decided, peering after several. They saved the rest of the sugar for bait and ran west. "I heard that a bee goes just about straight when he's on the way home, so let's move a few hundred feet more."

They stood in the open with the sugar smeared on a piece of bark.

"Here's one," Maud whispered. The bee dipped down and worked on the sugar, then zoomed away in the same direction the other had.

"We're on the right track." Jeff stumbled through the bushes and suddenly stopped, grinning apologetically to Maud, " 'Guess I've clean forgotten Carl's first law of caution about always being quiet."

An hour's slow work and a mile away from home they were led to a huge basswood tree. Bees! It seemed there were millions zipping back and forth, darting in and out of a tiny crack twenty feet up the broad trunk.

Jeff found a stone and thumped it against the trunk. When a hollow dull thud sounded he grinned, " 'Thought so.

Basswood trees sometimes rot out when they get old. This one is hollow and it makes our job easy."

"But how?" insisted Maud, picking a dead leaf from a tangled pigtail.

"We'll go back to the cabin and get the ax. I'll chop a hole through and we'll build a fire inside and cover it with green leaves. Smoke will filter up and make the bees groggy. Then I'll chop the tree down and the honey'll be ours."

Together they scooted through the woods, startling a cottontail as they went. They told Maud's parents about their discovery. A stock of honey would be a real wilderness treat.

"Bring all the pails and containers you can carry, Maud," Jeff called, with the ax in his belt and a pan of live coals from the hearth. The coals, he thought, would take less time than starting a fire with his flint.

Thus they prepared themselves, and within a half hour the fire was blazing in the chipped out hole of the hollow tree core.

"We're ready for the green leaves, Maud."

The leaves were piled on and the hole plugged. The smoke pushed upward and a wisp drifted from the hole above.

"Look, the bees aren't coming out any more, just going in," Maud announced.

"I guess it's safe to chop now." Jeff swung the ax. The basswood was soft and pithy and the ax cut easily. When the tree began to quiver Jeff stood back, "Are many going in now, Maud?"

"Practically none." At her report Jeff continued. The tree tottered like an uncertain old man in a wind storm. With a grinding rush it swung earthward with a tremendous crash.

The tree split open halfway up the trunk. With a scream of delight Jeff and Maud saw a rich golden mass of honeycomb. Bees were all over, but they weren't at all active. Using flat chips from the tree they scooped the honey along with a few bees into the containers.

"Yowieee!" groaned Jeff, holding his neck where a bee managed to sink its stinger.

"I guess he doesn't like the idea of the raid," Maud laughed.

"The smoke is wearing off and they're coming to. Let's rekindle the fire again." This done, the work went on. The pails filled, but still more honey lay in the open trunk.

"Let's take this home and bring the bucket we milk Dolly in," Maud suggested.

Through the woods they went, each carrying a load of honey. They found three more containers, along with Dolly's pail. The second trip exhausted the supply. Mr. Watson estimated the treasure at well over a hundred pounds.

They sat around the table feasting on cornbread covered with honey, washed down with creamy milk.

"This is the tastiest feast I ever had!" Maud exclaimed.

"Oh say, I forgot my axe. I'll have to go back and get it," Jeff said.

"I'll go with you," Maud suggested.

"No, Maud, I'll go alone. I'll make better time and get back to help with the chores."

Jeff ran toward the tree and glanced for the axe. It wasn't there. He studied the ground. He circled about wondering if he had given the axe a careless toss. Suddenly he dropped to his knees.

"It's a moccasin track, smaller than mine and fresh. An Indian's been here!" He moved cautiously, picking out the trail as it led to the stream and then veered westward. He followed for a few hundred yards and then, seeing the long shadows of eventide, he retraced his steps and picked up the Indian's trail before it came to the tree.

It led in a roundabout way back to the cabin. He

discovered a place in the woods in full view of the Watson family, where the Indian had hidden.

Trembling with excitement, he called Mr. Watson and showed him where the Indian had been. "Was there only one?" the missionary asked.

"Yes, but he probably is a scout for a larger band, and even now he might be leading the others toward the house," Jeff told him, remembering how Carl Ives described their ways.

"Quick then, let's move into the cave!" They ran to the house and told the others. Moving with a swiftness, born of necessity, the windows were taken out and hidden. The food stuffs were lowered to Maud who was at the bottom of the ladder in the hideaway. The blankets and cooking utensils with all the other items were cleared.

Jeff shoved the wagon down the slight hill to the stream where he let it disappear into a deep hole of water. He led Dolly and the yoke of oxen off into the woods and slapped their flanks, chasing them off. Better to risk them in the woods than let the Indians slaughter them.

Hurrying back to the cabin, Jeff found it as he first saw it, barren and empty. Mr. Watson was bringing up his third load of water from the spring for a safe supply.

Jeff entered the hole in the floor last, pulling over the flat stone that hid its secret. In the cave they made themselves as comfortable as they could in the darkness.

"We are in the Lord's hands, so let us not grow frightened. He has promised us the protection of the shadow of His wings, like a mother hen caring for her chicks. No matter what, remember that," Mr. Watson spoke softly and earnestly.

"It was surely the Lord's doing that led Maud and Jeff to that bee tree. And it was the Lord who made Jeff forget his ax. If he had not, we would not have known of the red-skin," Mrs. Watson added.

Jeff spoke, "I'm thankful such a wonderful scout as

Carl Ives showed me how to track. If it hadn't been for him, I never could have done it."

"As long as everyone is thanking the Lord for something," Maud joined in, "I will also. I thank the Lord for Jeff finding this cave and also for the hundred pounds of honey we have."

Without any further talk Mr. Watson asked the Lord to care for them. When he said "Amen" Jeff told the others: "I'm going up and watch from the opening. There's still a little light and they might get here before dark."

Mr. Watson said, "I'll come with you."

From the opening they could see the cabin directly below them; the corn field and the vegetable plot, the brook running lazily, and they saw something else that concerned them. Dolly the cow was walking out of the woods toward the corn.

"We can't risk chasing her, for fear the Indians will find our hiding place," Mr. Watson said.

Dolly ranged up to the cabin door, sniffing curiously. Jeff found a loosened rock and tossed it down. His aim was perfect. The rock hit her bulging side. With a dissatisfied snort she swung about and reentered the woods. At least one crisis was gone. The sunlight tinted the tree tops with a golden amber. A robin sang from a maple tree.

Darkness came with no signs of raiders. When they couldn't see any more, Jeff and Mr. Watson crawled back to the others and curled up for the night.

Several times Jeff awoke, listened carefully, and hearing nothing returned to sleep. It was Pam stirring and calling baby-like that announced sunrise. But as far as they were concerned it could have been midnight, for it was sooty dark in the cave.

Jeff wormed his way to the opening and glanced around. A heavy mist still clung over the fields and stream, but the sun glinted into his eyes from the east. Overhead the blueing sky promised a clear day. Carefully he scanned the woods, but saw not a thing to arouse his attention.

"As calm and peaceful as a sleeping kitten out there," he reported to the others.

"After we eat, I'll go up and watch with you," Mr. Watson said.

Maud chipped in with a "Me too!"

"Mother, it looks as though you'll have to stay back here with Pam. I certainly hope she is quiet," Mr. Watson said.

Breakfast consisted of honey-covered johnnycake and milk. Mr. Watson quoted the Twenty-Third Psalm.

When they stationed themselves, peering out into the bright light, it was about eight o'clock. Not a breath of wind stirred the corn. The water in the stream was still, without a ripple breaking the surface.

"I hope Dolly and the oxen won't drift near," commented Maud.

Two hours passed. Maud asked, "Do you think they're coming? Maybe after all that one Indian was alone."

"They don't travel alone, Carl Ives said. I just know that redskin was a scout and I feel sure we'll see them before the day is out. This cabin stood through several raids, and now that they have discovered it, they won't let it stand," Jeff replied.

A blue jay screamed to the west. Jeff whispered, "Carl told me to always find out what a blue jay or a crow is scolding about when they call like that. It could be the Indians startled him."

13

"It's Safer Here"

JEFF STUDIED the west bank of wood rising like a wall beyond the swaying corn. He heard the shrill squeal of a chipmunk, saw it flash up a tree and knew something was close.

A bronzed hand moved aside a low hanging branch. A painted face, yellow, with large circles around the eyes giving them a strange owlish appearance, stared from among the leaves.

"Look!" Jeff breathed. Maud and her father followed his glance. Maud drew her breath in sharply and gripped his arm for a moment, releasing it immediately.

The Indian studied the cabin for five minutes and beckoned to someone behind him. A white man pushed his head close to the redskin's and peered at the building.

Jeff took his eyes from the two figures and studied the woods. Ten feet farther away another face showed, then another, until he could make out five. Maud and Mr. Watson were also aware of them and Maud slipped back in the tunnel. Jeff knew she was going to tell her mother.

At least a half hour passed with the raiders still as trees. Finally the white man's face disappeared and another Indian pushed up.

"Look, Jeff. They're starting a fire." Jeff saw a tiny swirl of smoke drifting toward the tree tops. The Indians were growing bolder. One stepped into full view and then darted back to the fire. A moment later he reappeared with a long arrow strung to his bow. The arrow was tipped with a wad of dry grass blazing bright.

The Indian crouched, aimed and let the arrow fly. It fell ten feet short. Another Indian appeared with his bow drawn, arrow ablaze. The arrow clattered on the bark roof and dropped off.

Then three warriors stepped out. Their arrows flew. One landed on the roof, the others fell harmlessly on the packed earth near the door. But one was enough, the roof caught. A hopping blaze leaped and crawled slowly upward.

Maud returned and almost gasped aloud as she saw what had happened. Jeff pressed his hand over her lips.

They watched the blaze play along the roof like some grotesque yellow monster. Jeff tingled with anger. Why burn a cabin, reduce it to a heap of ashes, when it took so long to build!

The flames grew, bounding like hundreds of little crazy monsters, sending up flying black ash toward the blue sky.

A section of the roof caved in and the fire raged in earnest. Nine Indians stepped within a hundred feet, each armed with a musket. *Probably,* Jeff thought, *muskets sold to them by the traitor, Kittle.*

Jeff knew the Indians were waiting to see if the settlers were in there; waiting to kill and murder if the fire drove them out. With a shudder he wondered what might have happened if he hadn't found the cave.

The logs were blazing, sending up waves of heat and glowing fragments. It burned his eyes, and his nose began to sting, but he couldn't tear his gaze from the destruction below.

More Indians came from the woods, thirty-two in all. Then Jeff saw four white men step out, and one of them was the fat jowled Kittle. They watched the fire until the sides caved in, leaving only a few logs, black and desolate, to show where a home had been.

"They must've gotten word about us coming!" a tall man called.

Kittle grunted, "If they were in there they musta' felt a little warm. It's too bad. I promised these redskins a few scalps for their trouble." Jeff felt the blood rise to his tingling cheeks. He wondered how anyone could be so fiendish.

"Hey, tell them friends of yours to scout around and see what they can find," the tall uniformed man ordered.

Kittle called to the Indians, translating the orders into the Mohawk language. With a queer, chilling shout the Indians set off.

At that very moment one of the oxen walked into the clearing, bellowing at the smell of smoke. The Indians leveled their guns; at least twenty shots broke the air. The ox slumped forward.

The loud report must have frightened Pam, for Jeff heard the baby's cry away back in the cave. He watched the men below, praying they hadn't heard. But he knew they couldn't, for the Indians' shrieking cries roared above Pam's plaintive voice.

The Indians swarmed toward the fallen animal and with flying tomahawks they cut the hide and began to slash off hunks of meat.

"I guess we're in luck," Kittle laughed, "with their bellies full those idiots won't be so hard to handle. Let's go over there and get some for ourselves."

The white men walked over and at a word from Kittle the redmen backed away from the carcass until the Englishmen had what they wanted. They speared the steaks with pointed sticks and crowded around the still smouldering fire and roasted the meat. Jeff hoped against hope Dolly and the other ox wouldn't put in an appearance.

When the feast was done the Indians squatted off to one side by themselves, some chattering in their own tongue, while others slept, curled dog-like on the ground.

The white men sat on the bench under the maple, their voices drifting to where Jeff and Mr. Watson strained to hear.

"Kittle, tell them to burn the corn field," ordered the tall officer.

The fat man complied. Three Indians found flat stones and scooped up glowing ashes and tossed them against the first row of stalks, but the corn was far too green and wouldn't catch fire.

"Praise the Lord!" Jeff heard Mr. Watson mutter.

"It's no use, Captain," Kittle said.

"Well, they probably won't risk their necks coming back here after we get done with the raid."

"Say, it's getting late. If you plan to surprise Killypox we'd better move on." A short squat man made the suggestion.

"I doubt if this family knew how strong we are. They probably just got a little nervous and decided to go to the fort for a visit. Anyway, there's no use trying to move these Mohawks with their bellies as full of meat as they are. I say let's go back to last night's camp and get an early start in the morning," Kittle told the others.

"I'm for that, I'm so tired I don't care who wins this rotten war. I wish I were back in London right now." It was a short man complaining in a high voice.

Agreeing, Kittle passed the word to the Indians. They stirred from where they lounged. One big husky brave picked up a stick and walked toward the charred ruins. He poked the ashes, found a forgotten pewter cup, pounced on it and yelled in surprise when he touched the hot metal. He blew lustily on his burned hands. Another Mohawk balanced the cup on the tip of a stick and ran to the stream, plunging it in with a happy cry.

Then he shouted again and the whole band ran down to the brook edge. He pointed to the deep hole where Jeff had sunk the wagon. With a shriek, several leaped into the water. Desperately they hauled and tugged at the hickory tongue, but the wagon stayed where it was, for the right hind wheel was jammed between two boulders.

From the cave opening Jeff almost shouted his derision at the defeated plan to ruin everything they saw.

They returned to the fire, poking around with renewed interest, hoping to find more forgotten cups. One brave dug in the ashes directly above the stone that hid the secret cave entrance. Mr. Watson turned to Jeff and breathed, "If he discovers it, we're done. I'm going down to Mary and the children."

The Indian explored curiously, and then forgot himself. He stepped on the ashes and screamed as the heat burned through his thin moccasins. The others roared in laughter as the howling warrior dashed to the stream and plunged his feet in the water. His investigating was forgotten.

"All right, Kittle, dispatch two scouts to Killypox. Tell them to see how many armed men are there and report as soon as possible. Order the rest back to camp immediately," the Captain said.

The ponderous traitor translated the commands and the band disappeared to the west. Jeff darted down to the Watsons and related the narrow escape.

"That warrior's going to have sore feet for quite a while. You should have seen the way he hobbled after the others; like a man walking on a field of porcupines."

"I'm glad the Lord made the fire hot," Maud said in the darkness.

"Say, if that band is planning to raid tomorrow we ought to let the fort know about it!" Jeff exploded.

"Do you suppose we could all get through to Killypox?" Mrs. Watson asked.

"It would take too long," Mr. Watson answered.

Jeff already had decided what he thought best and expressed himself, "I know the way, and I can go alone. If the Mohawks find me I think I could outrun them. Besides, the Indians, knowing this cabin is burned, aren't likely to come this way again, so it's safer here than it would be at the fort."

Reluctant as Mr. Watson was to the plan, he saw Jeff's well-taken point. Mrs. Watson fixed food for him and within ten minutes he wiggled up to the opening and down the steep slope, pausing only a moment at the bottom to gaze in sorrow at the ruins.

Immediately Jeff went to where the two Indian scouts were last seen and picked up the trail; an easy one to follow. It was puzzling for a while to see the tracks unconcealed, but probably they were tired, full of ox meat, and perhaps a bit angry with being sent on a mission when the others had a chance to rest, Jeff thought.

From the position of the sun, he thought it to be about four thirty; plenty of time to reach the fort before dusk. He bent to the task of the moccasin prints and threaded his way after them for two miles. They came to the foot of a steep mountain and veered off eastward, skirting the rise.

"I could save two miles by going over it instead of around. Those redskins will probably put up for the night, so I probably won't run into them."

Jeff abandoned the tracks and plunged up the forested slope. Breathless and tired, he came to the crown where he sat upon a fallen log to rest. He turned and saw the last whisping smoke drift over the burned cabin. To the south he saw the staunch log fort at Killypox, with the blockhouse, like a guard, rising about the trees.

Rested somewhat, he moved on. The way was easier going down hill and he paced himself to a trot the way Carl said would cover ground and yet not tire a body out in an hour.

14

"Carrying A Dead Pig"

THE SUN gave promise of another hour's evening light when Jeff passed the first settler's clearing. A spanking new cabin stood in the center of a field of corn. A woman waved from the door and three children clung to her skirts and looked shyly at the stranger.

Jeff waved back, but didn't pause. The sight of the home sharpened his concern and he was tempted to warn the mother of the coming invasion, but thought better of it, "I'd best report to Captain Snow and let him give orders. There's still time before the attack in the morning."

Still trotting, he passed another cabin, and then an old burned heap in a brush-covered field, a silent monument to the treachery of the English, encouraging redmen to kill. Next to the ruins two crosses of hickory poles told where the settlers lay.

He broke into the clearing around the fort. It was a scene of bustling activity; men threshing grain, women sitting about, some with babies, others preparing for the evening meal. Boys were fishing in the river, and a number of others played under a pine tree.

A small black dog yapped a greeting at Jeff as he headed for the gate. The guard challenged him and his face showed recognition, "Oh, it's you again!"

"I must see Captain Snow at once," Jeff told him. It

was Lumberkin, the scout who had seemed intent in making life miserable for him.

"Maybe the Captain won't want to see you," the man leered.

"He must, it's important." Jeff started through the gate, but the man slashed at him with the gun barrel, "Not so fast," he growled, watching Jeff rub his left arm where the gun had glanced off.

Jeff stood still, eyeing the hostile man. Suddenly he bolted past Lumberkin, through the gate, and toward the blockhouse.

"Captain Snow, Captain Snow!" he shouted.

White whiskers followed by a sun-reddened nose poked through the blacksmith shop door. "Who's calling me?" boomed the buckskin-clad pioneer.

"Jefferson Lockwood."

"I told you to keep clear of this place!" Angrily the Captain strode toward him, the beard flicking outwards at every word.

"There's going to be a raid tomorrow morning."

"A raid?" · The voice was unbelieving, "A raid? How do you know? Is this some prank of yours?"

With a heart full of relief, Jeff spotted the tall black-haired figure of Carl Ives running toward him. A number of others, curious to see what the commotion was, gathered about them. Lumberkin bounded up and shouted, "You dirty little beggar!"

"Wait a minute," Carl called, then to Jeff, "What's the matter?"

"Indians came and burned the Watsons out. There were four white men with them. Kittle was there and we heard their plans to raid the valley early in the morning."

Carl interrupted. "Were the Watsons taken?"

"No, we escaped into—" he stopped short, not wishing to reveal the secret of the cave. Carl understood, for he filled the pause with another question. "How many were in the band?"

"Thirty-two, and the four white men."

Captain Snow snorted, "Carl, this could be a trick. Don't forget this boy's father is a Britisher."

Carl swung around and his voice took on a new tone, low and full of meaning. It gave Jeff a feeling of love he had never known for the man when he heard the words, "Captain Snow, this boy is a friend of mine. I'm not sure about his father, but I know him. He's telling the truth and if you're wise you'll sound the warning and bring in the settlers."

Slowly Captain Snow turned to one of the men. His respect for Carl Ives overruled his suspicions. "Kennon, ring the bell."

The man loped toward the blockhouse, up a ladder to where the bell hung. He lifted the steel mallet hanging by the side and sounded the warning. Three times the billowing tolls rolled out to the hills, echoing and re-echoing like high-pitched thunder.

From outside the men, women and children poured into the log barrier. Already their faces were taut with fear. As time went on the outlaying settlers came in on wagon and afoot, leading cows, carrying sheep, or tugging them on ropes.

Carl Ives led Jeff up the blockhouse ladder where they could see the activities from all directions. The people came, wondering and disturbed. Many of the women wept, holding their babies in their arms. Carl shuddered. "They began to think the war was over, Jeff. Many of them built new cabins where old ones had stood."

"Do you suppose the fort will be attacked?"

"I doubt it. We're well armed. Of course, you can never tell. If those white men can stir the warriors up they might. We'll just have to wait and see."

Late afternoon slid into dusk, dusk into gloomy darkness, and then pitch-black night settled over the fort. Carl said, "So that cave of yours saved the Watsons. I'm glad. We need men like him to proclaim salvation to the settlers. It's strange how easy folks forget there's a Saviour to lean upon. They get so tangled up with everyday living they don't take time to pray or read the Scriptures."

Captain Snow's booming voice stopped further talk, "Everyone is accounted for within five miles. As most of you know, there's been reported a band of raiders to the north heading this way. There's to be no fires and no further talk. Every able-bodied man is to take his accustomed position."

So the night settled into silence. Only the breathing of the men, a baby's occasional cry, or a yapping dog could be heard. Jeff stayed with Carl, peering through the black, listening for any strange noise.

Carl breathed in Jeff's ear as the sky paled the tiniest bit in the east, "Kittle will be ripping mad when they find the settlers are in the fort, and those Indians will be hard to control."

A shroud of misty fog clung to the river and around the fort when the light made seeing possible. The men grew tense, watching, watching — watching.

It was Carl Ives who shouted, "They're here!" Jeff saw two fleeting shadows creeping up behind a cabin. A volley sounded from the west side of the fort. A hideous scream carried to them from near the cabin. The nearest Indian flung his hands over his head and dropped lifelessly to the ground. The other turned and ran toward the woods, but a second volley tumbled him to earth.

"Look, behind that cabin!" Jeff shouted. A dozen red-skins had slithered, stomachs hugging the ground, through a cornfield and were running over a twenty foot clearing to protection. Guns barked, but the distance was almost out of range.

From the woods to the east a sprinkling of shots rattled

toward the fort. The bullets thudded into the log blockhouse, causing the men to use the loopholes for shooting.

Captain Snow came up, "Carl, how many do you figure? Seems like a heap more than thirty-two and four whites to me."

"I think you're right. Probably the band that burned Watson's was joined by another."

All day long the siege continued spasmodically. Then suddenly it was over. They waited for a long time, watching the still woods. Captain Snow ordered Lumberkin and Carl to scout the enemy.

"Captain Snow, I want to take Jeff Lockwood with me," Carl informed the man.

The white shaggy brows knitted in dissatisfaction. "Maybe," he finally concluded, "it would be better if he went with you."

"If he goes I ain't going. He's liable to lead us into a trap," Lumberkin whined.

"I don't blame you," snorted the Captain.

"You seem to have forgotten this boy saved this fort from total destruction by risking his neck in getting the warning through," Carl snapped.

Captain Snow laughed. "Maybe I did. Maybe I did. It does appear that he's the hero. Well, Carl, you take Lockwood along. I'll keep Lumberkin here."

They slipped through the gate and ran to the woods. "Just in case one or two of those redskins are waiting to take a pot shot at us," Carl laughed. Carl picked up the trail easily, headed east along the Mohawk. After studying the tracks he told Jeff, "There are about fifty Indians and at least a dozen white men." Making certain of the general direction the enemy was taking, Carl swung off the trail, "They always leave a few drifters back to see if they're being followed and they could ambush us if we plodded along in plain view."

As they moved Carl pointed out dozens of things of

interest. Once where a bear had scratched a tree; a tuft of rabbit fur showing where a fox had made a capture; another, where a deer had bedded down and countless other things.

"How can I ever learn it all?" Jeff wondered.

"It takes time, but you will. For that matter, you're better than Lumberkin right now, and after what you did the last few days I'm willing to take a back seat."

Four miles they traveled before the smell of smoke caught their attention. "They've made camp," Carl said. "Now we do some stalking. I'll lead. If anyone sees us, don't stop a second, but run; run like you've never run before."

Using underbrush and trees for cover, the two figures eased close to the camp in a ravine. An overhanging ledge afforded them a good position and they lay side by side looking down at the unsuspecting men. Kittle was there, all three hundred pounds of him, sitting half asleep by a fire.

"That Indian there by the horse —" Carl breathed, "that's the most fabulous of them all. His name is Joseph Brant, a name never to be forgotten as long as the Mohawk Valley is remembered. The odd part about it is that I believe he's a Christian although I can't be sure."

Jeff whispered, "Why is he with the British?"

"Well, for years they've heard that loyalty to England was almost as important as worshipping the Lord, so when the Revolutionary War started five years ago he gave his loyalty and services to them."

Carl counted the men and slid back into the woods. By the time they had traveled a mile the sun went down. The sight of Joseph Brant lingered in Jeff's mind's eye.

Almost as though he knew Jeff's thoughts, Carl said as they walked, "Joseph Brant's father was a pure blood Mohawk; his mother, although I'm not positive was partly white. He can speak English better than you and I. In fact, he has translated the Gospel of Mark into the Mohawk language. I guess you can't blame him too much for fighting the pioneers. After all, this was the land of the redmen before the whites came. Brant hates to see the country cleared, hates to see his people driven out. Oh, how I wish this war would stop! Hundreds have been scalped in this valley by his men, and this summer is worse than ever."

Thoughtful silence engulfed Jeff. Not another word was spoken until they reached the fort and were admitted after identifying themselves.

"Did you find them, Carl?" Captain Snow boomed.

"We did, Captain, and Joseph Brant is with them, which sorta' leads me to believe there's a swarm of others nearby. This may be that raid we heard was to come this year."

Jeff fell asleep almost as soon as he curled up in the blacksmith shop. Carl awoke him before dawn. "A scout from thirty miles to the east just came in. He tells of about eight hundred Indians moving through the valley. What we saw was only part of a larger group, as I suspected."

"Shall I tell the Watsons to come to the fort?" Jeff asked, slipping into his moccasins.

"No, I believe they're as safe there as here, Jeff. I'd go back with you, but I'm needed here."

Carl waved goodbye as Jeff slipped into the wilderness after a hurried breakfast. During the night a thunderstorm had cleared the air. The dampness made the burned cabins he passed look even blacker and more desolate than he imagined possible, with only the fieldstone chimneys standing gaunt against the sky.

Three miles from where the Watsons were waiting in the cave, Jeff saw a moccasin print in the rain-soaked earth. His first thought was to return and tell Carl of this new discovery. They had thought all the raiders were moving east and here were prints leading north.

He followed the prints for a short way and then noticed a red blotch on the leaves. "Probably carrying a dead pig or a sheep he's stolen from the settlers," Jeff thought. He followed a hundred yards and began to suspect the Indian was struggling under a heavy load, for the trail showed where something had fallen to the earth and bled before the prints led onward.

At each step Jeff paused and searched the woods about him. No telling where it might lead. Yard by yard he advanced, until he saw something laying half hidden under a low-limbed spruce. He studied it for a full two minutes before he made out the legs of an Indian.

Cautiously he edged forward, using trees for protection against any trick. The entire body was now in view. The Indian was laying, face down, with outstretched arms.

On the right shoulder a spot showed bright red against the flesh. Beside him lay a quiver of hunting arrows and a bow. A half hour Jeff waited; then feeling certain it was no ambush, he walked forward.

At first he thought the Indian was dead, but searching for the pulse he felt a slow beat. Puzzled, Jeff wiped off the blood. What could he do now? To leave the Indian would mean death for the warrior. To take him back to the stockade meant about the same thing, for the settlers were furious with the raiders and would be quick to kill. Only one thing to be done, he decided, carry the Mohawk to the Watsons.

15

"Sorta' Risky"

THE BURDEN JEFF CARRIED on his shoulders made the way hard and tedious. Time upon time, he eased the unconscious Indian to the ground and rested. Each time he felt the pulse, found it still beating, and struggled onward.

Midafternoon found him within shouting distance of the Watsons. Thankfully he laid the man beneath an oak tree and walked on alone.

"Hello, Jeff!" It was Maud who called from the cave opening. The ashes below gave a grim, forlorn appearance to the place. Dolly, her bag caked and sore from lack of milking, bellowed a greeting. The ox was in the cornfield gorging himself on the tasty ears.

With a shout, Jeff waved and chased the ox at the same time. He ran to the heap of ashes and brushed aside the rubble from the stone, lifting it and dropping it as quickly as possible.

"Jeff, am I glad to see you back!" Mr. Watson's voice came from the darkness. After the warm greetings were over, Jeff described his adventures, telling of the seige and of seeing Brant and the raiders. When he told them of finding the Indian, Mr. Watson nodded, "You did right Jeff. That Mohawk has a soul, and perhaps it's the Lord's opportunity to reach him with the Bible."

"We can't bring him here because we don't want the secret of the cave discovered."

"Well, let's go to him first, and see whether we can patch him up," Mr. Watson and Jeff left the cave and returned to the wounded man.

"He might not live," Mr. Watson announced, after a brief examination. "He has lost a great deal of blood."

"I'll go get some food and water for him," Jeff said. He built a fire nearby and made a broth of dried deer meat and poured it through the man's pinched lips. After four feeble swallows the eyes flicked open a moment, closing immediately.

"Jeff, we can build a leanto out here for him. Then if, and when he regains consciousness he won't be able to see our place."

So they worked until night fell. A rough pine bough structure was erected and the still figure laid on a blanket inside. Back at the clearing, Jeff tried to milk Dolly. The milk was thick and had to be thrown away, but the cow seemed not to have been permanently injured by the experience.

"Carl said he doubted if we would see the raiders since they have destroyed the cabin. This place is so far out of the way he thinks it's actually safer than the fort," Jeff told the family between munches of crushed corn and honey.

"Perhaps we could erect a makeshift shanty over the secret entrance so we could get a bit of sunshine. Pam is fretting here in the dark all the day long," Mrs. Watson said.

"We could attempt it." Jeff hesitated, thinking of the risk. "Of course, if there was another raid the secret might be discovered and besides, that redskin out in the woods could turn on us if he gets well."

"Let's try," Mr. Watson decided.

The next morning they found the Indian still and quiet, with eyes closed, but breathing steadily. More broth was poured between his lips and the wound wiped out. There they left him to return to the new venture.

A shell framework, fifteen feet from side to side, was erected of thin pliable saplings bound together by strips of willow bark. Then pine boughs were cut and woven in between the saplings. There were no windows, but an opening in the front let in light and air. The roof was covered with bark as had been the cabin, to ward off the rain.

The third day after Jeff's return, Mr. Watson and he arrived at the leanto where the Indian lay. As they approached they saw his eyes open.

"Our patient is improving," commented Mr. Watson, as he knelt beside the redman.

Jeff leaned over. The wounded man's face was fuller, with a rich bronze color that hadn't been there before. The Indian gazed steadily at them. His lips parted and in perfect English he spoke, "You will kill me?"

"No, we shall not kill you. We will nurse you back to health," Mr. Watson replied.

The man fed himself for the first time, closed his eyes and slept without another word.

"Mr. Watson, maybe we had better tie him up now that he's getting better so fast." Jeff suggested.

"Jeff, do you really think it's necessary? I hate to leave him out here bound hand and foot."

"But Mr. Watson, I can't help but think of Maud and Pam." Reluctantly the missionary agreed and the Indian was tied securely.

At dusk that evening they found the warrior awake. After he downed milk and johnny cake, Mr. Watson pressed questions. "Where did you learn English? What is your name?"

Carefully the answer was spoken, "I went to Samuel Kirkland's mission school near Fort Schuyler. My name is Wigo."

"Were you on that raiding party that attacked the fort?"

"Yes, that is where I was injured. I tried to return to

H

my village, but my blood ran freely. I grew tired. I fell down. I remember nothing more until I see you."

"Yet you fight against the people Mr. Kirkland loves?"

"Joseph Brant told us we must. The white man is taking what belongs to our people. We are driven from the land of our fathers'. It is not right."

The Indian answered a few more questions and then fell into a moody silence. Jeff replaced the cords of rawhide around the slender wrists and ankles and he with Mr. Watson, left for home.

In the days that followed the Indian gained in strength. Mr. Watson would go for several hours every morning, loosing the bonds so the Mohawk could exercise and flex his arms and legs. On all these journeys the missionary took his Bible with him and explained the Christian faith in detail, showing the Indian how everyone was guilty of sin before the Lord.

"And," he continued, "there must be punishment for these transgressions. So the Lord Jesus Christ took upon Himself our sins. He gave His life upon the Cross. He was buried, but no grave could hold Him. He arose, and even now is at the Father's right hand. If by faith you accept this truth you shall escape punishment and be saved."

The Indian expressed interest, but when the question of his personal belief came up he would doggedly reply, "I must think about it more."

Carl Ives drifted in one day late in the afternoon. He admired the new home and looked over the crops. "Mr. Watson," he said, "You can thank the Lord you got your crops in late. They were still green and wouldn't burn. The other settlers all along the valley are ruined. The cornfields were burned, hay stacks went up in smoke, hundreds of cabins are ashes, and practically every cow is gone. The area around Canajoharie was wiped out; men, women, and children's scalps were taken by the scores."

After a little more talk, Mr. Watson said, "Say, Carl,

maybe we're doing something wrong, but Jeff found a badly wounded Indian on the way here after the raid. We patched him up and have him tied out in the woods a piece."

"Sorta' risky, I'd advise against it," Carl said, brushing the black hair back over his shoulders. "Let's see him."

As they walked toward the leanto Jeff and Mr. Watson described the Indian's remarkable ability to speak English and his interest in the Bible.

"It could be that he might turn out all right, but Joseph Brant has a tremendous hold on the Mohawks. It's a doubtful chance."

"What can we do then?" Jeff asked.

"Well, I could take him down to the fort and when the next party of militia heads east they could take him to the prison in Albany."

At the Indian's side Carl asked, "Could you walk for a very long distance?"

"Yes."

"I plan to take you to the fort and from there you will be moved to Albany and put in prison until the war is over."

The Mohawk took the words without a trace of emotion. It seemed to Jeff he had expected something like this.

"We'll leave in the morning," Carl said.

Carl joined the group in the cave when night fell. He and Jeff slept near the opening, while the Watsons stayed in their accustomed place further back.

Curled in the blankets, Carl asked, "Jeff, how would you like to come with me? I have Captain Snow about convinced you're all right."

Jeff asked, "Would there be an opportunity to search northward for my father if I did, Carl?"

"No, Jeff, just routine work about the fort."

"Then, I'd better stay. The corn will soon be ready for harvest, and so will the beans, and Mr. Watson needs help. They've been so wonderful to me."

"I suppose you're right," the scout agreed.

"Carl, it's been almost six months since I left Albany in search of my father. Up to now, the only thing I've heard of him was what they said at Fort Killypox, and I feel as though I'm wasting my time."

"Not a single thing has come to my ears. It's hard to tell you what to do about going to search for him with conditions the way they are."

"Do you suppose this war will ever stop?"

"That's a question everyone wants answered. This is the late summer of 1780. It's been raging back and forth since 1775. Both sides have won victories with the balance of successes swinging to the English."

"George Washington has done more than anyone, hasn't he?" Jeff asked.

"Yes, I think so. Of course he lost New York, but he only had a handful of men. Then he had that terrible winter at Valley Forge two years ago in 1778. Another one like that would ruin the Continental Army."

"Well, at least Burgoyne lost over five thousand men for the English at Saratoga Springs."

"That might have been the only thing that saved total defeat. That, plus the militia battling away here against the English and Indians in this valley."

"If St. Leger hadn't been defeated at Fort Schuyler under General Herkimer, I guess we'd all be scalped by now." Jeff shuddered at the stories he had heard of the Wyoming massacre.

The two friends talked until late into the night. At dawn Carl prepared to leave for Killypox with the Indian.

Mr. Watson spoke, "Wigo, I trust you will remember what I have told you about the Lord Jesus Christ. I will be praying you will receive Him as your Saviour."

The Indian gave no reply but walked behind Carl Ives as the scout led the way into the forest.

16

"Hide Everything"

JEFF WORKED in the hot autumn sun harvesting the crops with Maud and Mr. Watson. A warm feeling of contentment grew with the heaps of golden corn. The beans, dry and hard, rattled as Maud shelled them into bark containers made for storing purposes.

Jeff laughed, "'Seems as though Pam realizes this bountiful crop means she won't be hungry this winter. Look at her playing with the corn cobs."

"Barring the unforeseen, it does appear as though we will get through the winter," Mr. Watson said, lugging beans down the ladder to the cave.

"In a few days we'll be able to gather nuts to help for winter meals," Jeff reminded Maud.

"These corn stalks, along with the wild hay we gathered, will taste good to Dolly and the ox."

"And with Jeff as our hunter, the table will be supplied with meat," Mrs. Watson smiled at Jeff who was hanging a bundle of corn with the husks peeled back, revealing the hardened kernels.

"I believe I'll be moving on as soon as the nuts are gathered. If there is no hope of going north to find my father, I'll have to return to Mother and Sis in Albany."

The announcement sobered the family. No one spoke until Mr. Watson asked the Lord's blessing at the evening meal. Jeff dreaded the thought of leaving, for this family was as dear to him as his own. It would be hard to go, but go he had to.

The frost hit early in October, turning the maple trees a golden yellow, and the oak leaves as red as cardinals. The background of deep green pines brought out the brighter colors in glorious display. Beauty and loveliness were everywhere. Birds by the thousands swung southward on their mysterious yearly journey.

It was that morning that Jeff had an idea. He went to Mr. Watson who was chopping wood for the fire. "Mr. Watson, living in this leanto for the winter isn't possible. The cave will be far too cold, and the fort will be so crowded there won't be much space left. So while I'm still here, why not let me help you cut logs for a new cabin. Then when the snow piles up enough to prevent Indian raids you could erect the home."

"Jeff, that's fine. We'll be forever indebted to you," was Mr. Watson's response to the suggestion.

"It's the other way around, Mr. Watson. When I first met you I was a Christian, but I didn't know much about it. Listening to your Bible studies, hearing you pray, and seeing your daily joyful life, has given me more than I could ever repay."

So the plans were made. Jeff and Mr. Watson cut and dressed logs, using the lone ox to do the hauling. Each log was notched and barked, ready for the raising.

"There, now it's done!" Jeff said, one brisk afternoon, with a cold biting wind whipping down from the north. They scattered the logs to forestall burning if raiders attacked, but all were in easy distance of the building site.

The nuts were gathered, bushels and bushels of them; black walnuts, hickory and butternuts in plenty. "I'll try to get a buck for you folks," Jeff announced the next morning. "Then I think I'll see Carl and lay plans for leaving."

With his musket loaded and a jacket as protection against the snapping wind, Jeff followed the brook through the almost leafless trees. He walked only a mile, when he found the heavy tracks of a deer, freshly made, he knew, because the impressions were clear and sharp.

The trail was easy to follow, swinging north and then veering eastward up the mountain that lay in back of the Watsons'. Two other sets of tracks joined the larger ones.

Working slowly he tested the wind. "Perfect," he muttered, feeling it blow from the east.

Twenty minutes later he saw a motion far ahead. He studied the forest and made out the russet-colored coats of browsing deer. There were three of them. One huge antlered buck and two graceful hornless does.

The distance was far too great to chance a shot, so Jeff used a shallow gully for cover as he crept towards the game. From time to time he raised his head to see the deer and to test the wind.

One of the does bedded down, but the other two stood uncertainly, sniffing the air curiously. The gully petered out, the ground ahead was level, only trees afforded cover and Jeff still had to go at least twenty yards for a shot.

He tummied along the ground, lifting dried leaves and sticks as he went. A sound now would spell defeat. Ten yards covered, and the deer still stood. The other doe laid down, the buck swung his head and gazed soulfully in Jeff's direction, sniffing the air. Even from that distance he could hear the snorting sound of indrawn breath.

The buck began to walk further away, ten feet, fifteen, then he stopped, circled around the doe and edged straight toward Jeff's hiding place. A prayer for success filled Jeff's mind as the deer paced closer.

Carefully he cocked the musket and slowly worked

into position until the sights outlined the heart. Closer—
closer—*Now!* With a tremendous leap, the buck fled.

Discouraged, and almost unbelieving, Jeff leaped to
his feet, watching the deer disappear. It had been such an
easy shot, but he had failed.

He reloaded, walking toward the place where the buck
had stood. He searched the ground and found a tuft of
blood-spattered hair. Somewhat encouraged, he set out after
him. As he went, he noticed an increase in size of the blood
patches.

Two miles away he found a small pool of blood where
the buck had rested a moment. The tracks swung south in the
general direction of the Watsons'. The blood spots grew
smaller and then disappeared. "A flesh wound, probably," Jeff
thought sadly.

He scanned the woods ahead, stopped short when he
saw something move, and heard a hollow grunt, so unlike
a deer that Jeff was surprised. He eased forward, foot by
foot, seeing once again the motion beyond a pine tree. It
wasn't the rich brown coat of a deer, but a stubby-legged
animal as black as the inside of the cave.

In astonishment, Jeff saw a huge black bear rear on its
hind legs, lower again on all fours and shuffle away. With the
musket ready, he wormed his way through the trees. The
bear had stopped and was pawing something in the leaves.
Jeff fired. The bear let loose a fearsome bellowing howl. The
gun reloading seemed to take an hour. He aimed again and
fired. The bear gave a nasal whoop and toppled over.

Running forward, Jeff loaded again, but there was no
need. The bear was dead, but another surprise lay in store
for him. The buck deer was not more than ten feet away,
stretched out, with legs extended, as dead as the bear.

"Wowiee!" exclaimed Jeff as he bent to the task of
cleaning the animals. He carried as much meat as he could
back to camp. Mr. Watson and Maud returned with him and

helped, until all the meat was safely stored for smoking. Mrs. Watson was delighted with the vast quantity of fat on the bear.

"I'll make candles with that tallow. Then we can have a little light at night."

At noon Mr. Watson went to the stockade and Mrs. Watson took Pam for a walk along the stream. Maud squatted before the leanto and worked on a new set of birchbark dishes for the family. Jeff was beside her, patching his worn moccasins and mending his buckskin jacket.

"Jeff, I'm about out of bark. I think I'll go down to the birch grove and cut some."

"I'll go, Maud," Jeff started to scramble to his feet, but the girl shook her head.

"No, you stay here. It will only take an hour and I'll enjoy walking. It's so brisk and nice out this afternoon."

Jeff watched Maud disappear into the forest, then returned to the task of mending and patching. His mind was still confused about the future. "If I have to return to Albany and tell Mother and Sis that 'most everyone believes Dad turned traitor, it will break their hearts. Yet, as surely as I sit here, there must be an answer to the riddle."

Jeff finished the repair work and idly carved a chunk of cedar into a bear for Pam. "This wild New York territory has won me completely. When all this clears up I'm coming back here. Carl has said that someday after the war, new towns and cities will spring up along the river. Fortunes will be made from the water power; farms will thrive on the fertile bottom land, and the lumbering industry will boom. Any one of these could occupy a fellow for a lifetime, and yet I'm not sure just what my part in the conquering of the wilderness will be."

He was carving the blunt nose of the cedar bear when Mrs. Watson returned with Pam. "Where's Maud?" she questioned.

Jeff replied, "She went down to the birch grove to cut some more bark. She should be back in a few minutes."

Pam toddled about in the dried leaves while Mrs. Watson sat on a bench. "Jeff," she said, "when do you think you'll leave?"

"I'm going to talk with Carl and see what he has to say."

"I'll be saddened to see you go. Why you've been like my own kin since we first met you."

"And I'll be sad in leaving, Mrs. Watson, but leave I must."

The shadows lengthened, the sun hung low in the deep blue fall sky, promising only a little more daylight. "I think I'll go and meet Maud."

"Perhaps she met her father and went with him." Mrs. Watson saw the bit of worry troubling Jeff.

"I don't think so, for Mr. Watson left long before Maud did." With a wave to Pam he followed the stream, picking out Maud's tracks here and there. He came to the grove and found where Maud had cut bark and had heaped it in a tiny neat pile at the base of a birch tree.

He called, but there was no answer. "That's funny. There's another pile of bark. She must be near."

Again he called her name, but the only answer was the frightened chatter of a red squirrel. He hurried now, studying the ground. The tracks led up a sandy knoll. There he saw what he dreaded; the plain outline of an Indian moccasin beside Maud's.

"Captured by a Mohawk," he breathed.

Jeff flew for camp with the news, bolting into the leanto calling to Mrs. Watson.

"What shall we do?" she asked, after Jeff had explained the situation.

"I'll track her and try to stop the redskin before

he bands up with a big force," Jeff decided, hurriedly tossing dried corn, smoked meat and beans in his pack sack.

Suddenly, thundering hoofbeats clattered outside. Jeff rushed to the door and saw Mr. Watson on a borrowed horse, bearing down towards him. Flinging himself from the tired animal the man shouted, "Hide everything! Quick! We're all going to the fort. A gigantic force of redskins and English are headed this way from their last eastern raid."

With a dispairing cry, Mrs. Watson collapsed in her husband's arms, crying out, "Maud has disappeared! An Indian has captured her!"

"I'm going after her," Jeff announced, swinging the pack on his shoulder and grabbing his musket. "Mr. Watson, as soon as you can, tell Carl Ives to follow me."

"But what can you do against so many?" the missionary asked.

"I don't know, but I hope to find Maud before the Indian joins a larger force. I know he was alone this afternoon. Just keep asking the Lord to travel by my side."

Jeff retraced his steps to the shady knoll and found the tracks in the waning light. They led in a northwesterly course and for an hour he made hasty going.

Finally, the murky gloom of evening blurred the trail and he had to stop. A tall oak tree served as a lookout tower, and for half the night Jeff peered into the darkness, hoping the Indian would betray his whereabouts by lighting a fire.

"I suppose there's no use watching any longer," Jeff thought, easing his cramped, aching body groundward from limb to limb. "Perhaps he knows someone is on his trail. The best I can do is sleep, and awake refreshed for the morning run."

17

"Hand Me My Boots"

LONG BEFORE A HONKING FLIGHT of wild Canadian geese split the first sign of dawn, Jeff was impatiently waiting to take the trail. After scooping up a drink, he pushed on and within a half mile he saw where the Indian and Maud had spent the night. She had rested on pine boughs and scraped her initials in the soft earth. She knew someone would follow, and the sight of the letters spurred Jeff on. *They can't be more than a half hour ahead. I know I can travel faster, for Maud can't keep the Indian's pace*, Jeff thought.

The trail swung up a wooded rise, down a swampy gully, then hit a much used deer path. Somewhere far in front of him, a distant crack of a rifle snapped. Abandoning the trail, Jeff raced forward, thinking the Indian had shot a rabbit or squirrel for food. To the northwest he saw a hill. Dashing through the trees he gained the summit, hoping to see the Indian.

He reached the highest point, stopping short; in front of him was a huge expanse of water, stretching away to the west. The morning sun skittered the surface with millions of flickering, darting silver patches, tossing and billowing, always changing, never still.

"It must be Lake Oneida," Jeff figured, remembering once again the wealth of information Carl had given him.

His attention was caught by the rhythmic thumping of

an ax between him and the lake. He studied the country. Trees spread away on all sides, the only break was the shimmering water. A single wisp of smoke a quarter of a mile away beckoned him on, but he waited, wondering. If the Indian was still alone he would be afraid of lighting a fire. Then a shot, and the sound of an axe. These things puzzled him.

Another wisp of smoke made him glad he had not blundered on. The Indian had met the larger force.

Using every trick of scouting Carl had taught him, Jeff eased down the hill toward the fires. He scanned every tree and bush ahead, remembering how every roving band of Indians put out scouts to the four winds. It paid off, for he spotted a Seneca brave perched catlike on a fallen tree trunk, idly whittling a stick with a long knife that caught the sun on the blade.

Moving slowly and easily, Jeff bypassed the sentry to the south, and worked toward the camp where he could hear the general hum of distant voices. He thought of turning back for help, but from where would it come? In all likelihood, there were other bands of Brant's raiders; maybe at that very moment the fort was under fire.

He gave up the idea, squirming under a towering pine, thankful for the heavy branches that touched the ground on all sides, forming a protective tent. Footsteps came up behind him and he heard a voice. "I'm glad that's over. That valley is burned out for good."

Another man spoke, and Jeff recognized Jake Haynes, the traitor's voice, "I can't wait to get to Niagara, there's money waitin' there fer me."

"I never saw such a happy bunch of Indians," Jake's companion said.

"Give them savages houses to burn, and women and children to scalp and they're all right." Haynes was within three feet of Jeff as he lay motionless under the pine.

"They sure don't take many prisoners, do they?"

Jake Haynes answered, "No, it's easier to carry a scalp than feed a man. There's only three this time. Those two rangers and the girl that redskin brought in this morning."

At his words, Jeff felt the blood course through his veins. Perspiration bubbles wet his forehead. He strained to hear the next words as the men walked slowly on, but only parts drifted back to him, "I'm . . . buy. Maybe sell her," and that was all.

Niagara! Jeff thought. *Why, Niagara is a hundred and fifty miles west. If I have to follow that far I'll never get back this winter, even if I do manage to free Maud. I'll have to hang as close as I can to this outfit and at the first chance risk a try to rescue her.* Jeff also thought of the possibility of finding word of his father. From the very beginning he felt his father had been taken captive by the English. Yet, he wondered why, if Lumberkin were telling the truth, his father was seen going with the Indian band and the English, without being bound.

Pondering these thoughts brought small comfort to him. Occasionally Indians came into view, milling about, dragging wood for the fires that now scented the air with smoke. Then mingled with the smoke came the rich pungent smell of frying pork and boiling coffee. A wave of hunger engulfed him, and he chewed on the smoked deer meat he had brought with him.

After breakfast the party moved on. The trail was easy to follow. The only danger lay in being caught by the Seneca Indians who were lagging behind as rearguards.

At noon another brief stop was made and then the party swung due west, following a much used path through the country. A dark grey filmy cloud blotted out the sun. A brisk raw chill fanned the few oak leaves remaining on the trees. Flakes of snow slithered down as night closed in.

Fires sparkled in nineteen different places. Shadowed figures bent over them, some holding frying pans, some with pots, while still other men warmed themselves. Jeff shivered on the narrow ledge where he lay hidden. He saw the sentry come in and knew the army felt safe from pursuit.

Jeff peered from fire to fire in hopes of seeing Maud among them, but even though he thought he saw a girl, he couldn't be sure, and a moody gloom of discouragement dogged his thoughts.

Voices carried from the nearest fire. Most he couldn't understand, for it was in the Indian tongue. After the meal a voice, apparently belonging to the commander of the outfit, rang out with orders. The words were clear, "Tomorrow we break at dawn, moving to Niagara as you all know. At the other end of the lake we will meet Kilmer's bands and travel together. Those Indians who plan to leave the main body for their homes can come to me and be paid off in the morning. The rest of you will be paid at Niagara when we get there." When the man finished, an Indian interpreted the orders into his language for the benefit of the other Indians.

The voices ceased, the fires dimmed to glowing spots of red and the men huddled in the blankets near the warmth. Jeff wished he dared to creep down, but the sentrys were too numerous to risk the attempt.

It was the most miserable night Jeff remembered. He couldn't sleep at all; he was cold and the wet snow drenched him. He worried about the snow, for with the white background there would be more danger of his being seen in the morning. His fretting led him to prayer and he claimed the promise of the Lord as he remembered the Bible words, "I will never leave thee nor forsake thee."

Toward morning the snow changed to a misty rain and when the party moved on the woods were soaked and soggy with most of the snow melted.

At the west end of Oneida Lake, Kilmer's party joined them, making a total of over two hundred and fifty men, a quarter of them Englishmen, with other white men who had deserted America's fight for freedom; the balance were Indians, chiefly Senecas, from the Genesee Valley villages, and Mohawks who had long since given up their homes on the river banks to find new homes to the north.

In the confusion of the meeting of the two groups, Jeff was enabled to draw close without being seen. In fact, he almost risked walking boldly into the encampment, for he noticed several other youths about his age, dressed in the same buckskin outfits. He abandoned this idea when he thought of the uselessness of trying to get Maud away in daylight. So he stationed himself in a tall pine and watched.

The Indians lined up in disorderly fashion before a man who paid each one. Jeff correctly figured these would be the redskins who would leave the main band for their own villages. It was then he caught sight of a blanketed figure, but it wasn't an Indian. It was a honey-haired girl, with long pigtails flouncing down her back.

Jeff recognized Maud. A tall redskin was by her side. With his captive the red man turned and called three other Mohawk warriors. Together they walked away from the others taking a northerly direction. Jeff shuddered to think what might have happened if he had not seen them. "In all likelihood I would have followed the main army, never realizing Maud was not there."

He slid from the tree and boldly stepped from his hiding place. To go around the large group of men and try to pick the right trail from the many that led away might bring the search to an end. So the only way was to risk attracting notice by a daring move.

With a confident swing he walked through a band of Indians. Their heavy sweetish body odor reminded him of the fight on the wagon months before. He passed through unchallenged. An Englishman, squatted by a fire called, "Hey, boy, hand me my boots!"

Without a word, Jeff saw the boots drying near the

flames. He walked over, picked them up and deposited them at the man's feet and moved on.

Up ahead he saw Maud disconsolately trudging away with the four men. Jeff dropped back, walking as unconcerned as he could, although his heart beat like the rollicking drums that sounded from behind, calling the remaining men to strike out for Niagara.

He found a place on the trail, hidden from the main army, and slid into the woods and let the Mohawks gain ground until they were out of sight. He followed ten minutes later, easily spotting the tracks. They continued northward for about five miles. A spiral of smoke showed where their village nestled beside a small lake.

Jeff concealed himself under the roots of a large tree and waited till sundown. "Maybe tonight I'll have the chance to free Maud," he muttered. With that prayer on his lips he fell asleep.

When he awoke it was growing dark; the north star dimly glimmered from the pale sky. Off toward the Indian camp Jeff saw a rousing camp fire. "Probably the warriors are being welcomed home by their squaws," he thought.

When darkness came, he wiggled his way forward on his stomach. He came upon a bluff above the camp and found a narrow cedar covered knoll where he lay in easy view of the village.

i

18

"Stay Where You Are"

FROM HIS LOOKOUT far above the Mohawk Village, Jeff watched the Indians celebrate the return of the warriors. At last all was quiet and the great fire went out. He fell asleep until the sun changed the night into dawn. The sky, a gentle blue, gave promise of a cloudless November day.

While he took out the cold uninviting corn and smoked meat from his sack, Jeff's mind filled with thoughts. He knew that no one from the fort could ever trace him to the Indian village, for his tracks were mingled with hundreds of others. Even Carl Ives, who was by far the best scout in the New York territory, couldn't be expected to help.

Yet something had to be done. Maud had to be rescued. Jeff had heard of prisoners being killed when food became scarce. He had heard how the Indians would carry the bloody scalps to the English and sell them for a few dollars a piece. Yes, something *had* to be done.

In the distance a yellow dog yapped in front of the largest of four, bleak, flimsy bark houses that formed the village. The door, nothing more than a blanket fastened over an opening, was pushed aside. Three squaws shuffled out with their peculiar duck-like gait. One knelt and stirred the charred embers of the fire, another added wood, while the third fanned with a slab of bark. The fire smouldered, then burst into flame.

Two more squaws joined the three and together they worked about the fire. A large pot sent a tiny cloud of steam into the sharp air. One of the squaws shouted and even from where Jeff sat he could hear her thin voice. Almost immediately five warriors followed by a troop of children of all ages, pushed out of the lodge, rubbing their eyes in the bright light.

Amid a great deal of talking and waving of arms the Indians squatted around the fire, dipping their hands in the pot and licking the food from their fingers.

Jeff watched the action intently, hoping to catch a glimpse of Maud. But there was no sign of her. It seemed to him every living soul in the village was grouped around the warmth of the fire eating breakfast. This troubled him, for if the Indians he had seen with her had not stayed, it would mean leaving his hiding place in daylight in an attempt to pick up the trail.

After the meal was finished the Indians separated, the children to a game of tag, the men to the eastern sunny wall of the biggest lodge, and the women to curing several deer hides stretched on clumsy oval wooden frames. Only one of the squaws remained near the fire. She scooped a portion of cornmeal mush onto a birch bark plate and disappeared into the smallest lodge.

I hope that means Maud is in there and I hope the food isn't so bad she can't eat it, Jeff thought, shifting himself to a more comfortable position, moving slowly so as not to catch the sharp eyes of the Indians. *If I get caught it means my scalp and probably Maud's too.*

The squaw returned to the fire and refilled the birch bark dish and reentered the lodge. *Maud must be hungry,* Jeff supposed, *or perhaps there's more than one captive.*

Jeff studied the village bit by bit in an attempt to figure

out how to get to Maud. Besides the four buildings, there was an open shed-like affair where two scrawny horses were tied. Another bark framework appeared to be a place where meat was smoked. Two small lopsided sheds, open on one end, were filled with cornstalks and a third held dried corn still in the husks. Jeff saw one of the squaws go to it and fill a basket with ears.

Suddenly Jeff tensed, a twig cracked off to his left. He flattened himself against the earth and waited. Two Indian boys, about eight years old, were creeping toward him with small bows drawn taut, and arrows resting in position.

At first Jeff thought they had seen him for they worked their way in his direction, but when they stopped and sat down in the sun he knew they had not. But if they continued, they would come upon his pack half concealed under an overhanging stone. Then surely he would be discovered.

Breathless and tense from the possibility, Jeff again found himself talking silently, but earnestly, to the Lord, asking for help.

For twenty minutes the boys squatted in the sun, babbling away in the Mohawk language. He tried to piece together the drift of their conversation, but the gutteral sounds were as confusing as the chatter of a bluejay.

A chipmunk scampered over Jeff's motionless feet and darted toward the boys. They saw it and tensed; drawing their bows. Their faces, dark and thin, puckered in earnestness. Suddenly an arrow flew, and with a deadly whine hit the chipmunk square on the nose. With a terrifying shriek the boys leaped upon the dead animal. Only then did Jeff realize the boys were playing a game, a game that ended with the killing of a white man. With shouts of triumph they ran down the slope to the village. A group of children gathered around and cheered as they viewed the dead animal.

The day wore on; the Indian warriors kept shifting themselves to sunny spots as the cooler shadows caught up

with them, but they did no work. Jeff supposed it was because
they had just returned from war.

The women were constantly busy. Some ground corn
while others continued to work on the deerhides. One young
woman tended a baby who was tied on a board and bundled
in fur.

Several times during the day the Indian children wandered near Jeff in their game, and each time Jeff prayed and
each time they wandered off again, much to his joyful thanksgiving.

No one entered the lodges after breakfast until the sun
swung far to the west. It seemed almost like summer, although the trees were leafless and the grass had lost its green.

Jeff noticed the Indian woman, who had taken the
food, enter the lodge again. The blanket door moved a bit
and the woman emerged. Then another figure stepped out into
the sunlight.

"Maud!" Jeff muttered.

She was still wearing her dress, tattered and ripped by
the journey through the forest. Her buckskin jacket was
ripped on the left sleeve. The squaw led the girl to a hollow
grinding stone where they sat down, crosslegged, and took
rounded rocks and began to pound a handful of corn thrown
in the hollow.

After working the corn into fine meal, Maud stopped
and looked about her. Jeff could see the sun reflecting on her
honey colored hair when she took it down and rebraided it
while waiting for more corn to be brought to her.

Another woman approached and the girl flashed a
smile as some word was spoken. "Thank the Lord," Jeff
breathed, when he saw the smile. "At least she isn't being
treated badly."

One of the warriors rose to his feet and peered off
to the east. Slowly the others followed, standing in their dark
brown blankets and apparently listening. One of the yellow

dogs began to bark and then another, until the entire pack was barking and snarling.

The Indians made a quick dash for the bark lodge and returned, holding their muskets ready. One shouted to the women and children and they ran toward the woods. Maud was taken with them.

Hopefully Jeff watched, for there appeared to be only the five Mohawks in the entire camp and they looked pitifully weak. Jeff longed to see an American rescue party arrive. But this hope died quickly.

One of the Indians leaped atop the low hanging roof of the lodge, gazing eastward for a few minutes. Then he began to wave his hands to those below, shouting and laughing. The others relaxed, and leaned their muskets against a tree.

A shout brought the women and children from the woods. Maud returned to the hand mill and continued to pound corn into flour. Jeff saw her brush tears of disappointment from her eyes. She, too, had thought the approaching sounds came from rescuers.

The distant thumping of horses hoofs gave hint of the visitor's arrival. A moment later about thirty white men walked into the clearing. After them at least sixty Indians, Mohawks and Senecas, followed. All of them, white and bronze alike, seemed exhausted. They flopped listlessly in the sun while orders were given to the women to prepare food.

Suddenly a tall dark-haired man caught Jeff's attention. He was moving toward the spot where Maud labored.

Something about the man, even from that distance, made Jeff aware of a strangeness. He studied him as best he might. The unshaven face was half-hidden behind a black beard. The frayed uniform showed plainly it was English.

Jeff's pulse quickened. He grew tense. His thumping heart seemed to fill the air with booming as loud as tom toms. With a sickening gasp Jeff almost cried out in his despair. That man down there was his father! His father! Jeff felt ill.

He had to fight the impulse to leave his hiding place and dash down.

Now his father stooped by Maud and said a few words. Another man walked over, stopped a few seconds, and then wandered off. Again his father talked; it seemed to be a hurried, earnest conversation. Twice Jeff saw Maud glance around at the woods.

After five minutes his father walked away. From where Jeff stared in astonishment he saw Maud rub tears from her eyes with the sleeve of her jacket. Jeff, confused and stunned, tried to work out a course of action. Now he had seen his father with his own eyes and with the enemy; talking with them, and in their uniform, traveling with them. Perhaps he had fired shots that killed or wounded the Americans who were protecting their homes and struggling for freedom. Oh, the sorrow of it all! How could the family circle ever be complete again? How could this be forgotten? Surely the Lord wouldn't let this happen, yet, here it was, just as plain as the sunny day itself.

Several other English soldiers talked to Maud. One went to the village Indians and spoke for a few minutes. Jeff could see one of the Indians shaking his head vigorously in protest over some proposition, perhaps that of buying the girl.

Again Jeff's father talked to Maud. He saw the girl listening as she thudded the round stone down on the corn in the hollow.

Twelve more men and three Indians entered the village that now bustled with confusion and activity. Jeff watched with little interest, thinking only of his father and his apparent treachery. What could Jeff tell his mother and sister? Then there was Captain Snow's bellowing voice that had sneered contempt, and Lumberkin, the scout. Even now Jeff could hear their words, "Samuel Lockwood is a traitor!"

A careless plan popped into Jeff's troubled mind. It

had worked once, it might work again. He would tie his pack on his back and walk boldly through the mass of men and hide in the bark house where Maud had spent the night. If it worked, he would free Maud during the night and escape. If he failed, he didn't care. He couldn't go back home anyway, and tell what he had seen.

Four of the men with three Indians went off into the woods to the west, carrying muskets. Twenty minutes later a shot rang out, then another and another. The triumphant shout from those in the village puzzled Jeff until he saw the men return from the woods with two deer. The others crowded about the game and many hands skinned the animals while others brought the meat to the squaws who were working at the fire.

"With all the excitement down there I guess this is as good a time as any to test my plan," Jeff muttered. Leaving the musket underneath the tree, he struck out boldly, circling the edge of the village until he came to where the most people were collected. He stepped out into plain view and watched the skinning of the deer.

"Here, take this over to the squaws," a man shoved a slab of deer meat into his hands. Without a word, Jeff complied with the orders, hoping desperately he wouldn't come face to face with his father.

He had to pass Maud. Her head was bent over, re-filling the hollow stone with more whole corn. She glanced up. A gasp came to her lips. She began to struggle to her feet, but Jeff hissed in a low voice, "No, stay where you are. Don't let on you know me."

He passed on, dumping the meat by the fire and striding toward the house Maud had come from. No one paid the slightest attention as he pushed aside the blanket door and slipped through. For a moment he couldn't see anything, for the light was dim. In fact, the only light in the building was a few gleams that passed through the cracks in the bark.

19

"The Message"

JEFF WAITED JUST INSIDE the door until his eyes became accustomed to the dingy interior of the bark lodge. Several blankets were tumbled topsy turvy on heaps of straw piled along one wall.

A chared, darkened spot in the center of the building showed where a fire burned in cold weather. The only outlet for the smoke was a crude hole in the roof. On the wall opposite to where the Indians slept, dried corn was hanging on a rafter built for that purpose.

On the far end of the hall-like room two deer skins were stretched on drying racks, standing upright against the wall. *Behind them is about the only place I can hide,* Jeff thought.

He stepped toward the spot when a rumbling snort brought him up short. He whirled to see what made the noise. Another snorting grunt caught his ears. He peered to the dark corner and made out the heaving form of an Indian lying on a straw heap.

The Indian was sound asleep, much to Jeff's relief. It appeared to be an old man or woman, but the light was too poor to be sure. Long white hair framed the wrinkled face.

The commotion outside grew in volume. To see what the cause was, Jeff took his knife and cut a slit in the stiff elm bark. Working quietly, the opening allowed a stream of

133

sunshine to break through. Outside he could see the area around the fire. The men were pressing toward it, while the squaws handed out the cooked deer meat. Jeff's father strode into view and accepted a piece, and sat down not more than thirty feet away.

Again a wave of disappointment surged through Jeff. He saw his father take a tin plate from his pack and pass it to an Indian woman for a dish of corn mush. The man bowed his head for a fleeting moment and began to eat.

Confusion grew in Jeff's mind. "Surely there must be a reason for his being with the English. Yet, what possible reason could there be?"

Maud walked up to Jeff's father and gave him another piece of meat. She attempted to say something, but one of the braves spoke sharply to her. Jeff heard the words in gutteral English even above the hum of activity. "You go where squaws work and no come back."

Without a reply Maud walked off, and Jeff saw her face lined with worry and fear. His father's voice drifted to him asking the Indian to sell the girl.

Again the Indian's voice raised in sharp anger, "No, I have promised to sell her to friend of mine. Tomorrow he come. I glad, for she much trouble. Everyone want buy her."

Tomorrow! The word rang in Jeff's ear. Tomorrow! Then tonight would have to be the night of escape if there was to be one.

Shadows gathered. With the disappearing sun also went the warmth. English soldiers built fires, gathering around in small groups, talking and arguing.

Jeff took advantage of the fading light to cut a hole in the bark so he and Maud could escape, if, and when the opportunity came. He braced the piece in place so no one would notice, and then settled back to wait.

Two children burst through the blanketed door, wrestling and tumbling, and bounced onto a straw pile. Four others followed. Then a squaw entered, muttering something in Mohawk language. The children quieted instantly.

From his place behind the deerhide Jeff saw two more figures push through the blanket. At first he thought they were both Indians.

"I will not tie you tonight, you have been a good girl," an Indian woman said in stammering English.

Then Maud's voice came to his ears, "Thank you. You have been very kind."

"I like white sister. I hear Samuel Kirkland tell of your Lord God. Sometimes I think maybe Indian gods not good. Ever since we join with English everything bad. Maybe Indian gods angry. I don't know."

"I know you would find joy if you put your trust in the Lord Jesus Christ," Maud said.

"Maybe. I don't know."

Maud asked, "Where did you learn to speak the white man's tongue?"

"Before war I work for Jacob Custer's wife. She teach me. She dead now. Warrior take her scalp. Good days before war. Now bad days. Hungry and afraid. My husband killed. Now very sad days."

Jeff heard Maud say good night to the Indian woman. He looked from behind the deer skin, but it was so dark he could see nothing. Then someone lifted the blanket at the door and let in firelight for a moment. Jeff saw Maud not more than three feet from him, curled up under a blanket.

Finally everything was quiet. Jeff felt sure Maud had seen him enter the bark lodge. He hoped she would stay awake.

A bright moon appeared in the sky. A dog howled a few times and then all was dead still except for the snoring of the old Indian in the far end of the building.

Jeff whispered, "Maud."

The answer came startlingly close, "Yes" was barely loud enough to hear.

"Can you move around this deer skin?" Jeff breathed, "I have a hole cut here."

There was a silence for a few seconds and then the soft rustle of straw came to his ears as the girl moved toward him. When he felt her arm on his he pushed through the bark. A cool breath of air swept in. Moving slowly, he eased his pack outside and slipped through. Maud followed.

He studied the sleeping soldiers a while. Several snored. One stirred, sat up, poked the fire into a blaze, and leaned back again.

Off to the west Jeff heard the tread of the sentry walking back and forth. He knew there would be guards on every side, and they presented a threat to their escape.

He took Maud's hand in his and skirted the back of the lodge toward the east. A dog, lean and hungry, sniffed at his heels. Jeff reached into his pack and found a strip of deer meat. He tossed it to the dog and it lay down quietly to enjoy the treat.

He led Maud toward the woods and breathed a bit easier when they entered the protective cover. They stopped and listened. Footsteps. Footsteps coming directly toward them.

In the dull pale light of the moon Jeff saw the glint of the sentry's musket barrel held loosely in the crook of the soldier's arm. With leisurely strides he came on, closer and closer, his tall figure swinging freely as he walked.

Quite suddenly he stopped, ten feet off; his gun swung around in readiness. He seemed aware of their presence, yet Jeff knew they hadn't been seen.

The sentry called softly, "Is someone there?"

With a quivering rage of emotion Jeff recognized his father's voice. Stunned, and completely swept off guard, he couldn't speak. Now the man saw them, the gun leveled.

Maud spoke, not loudly enough to be heard by the other guards. "It's the girl you were talking to this afternoon. I'm escaping."

The man stepped closer. "Who's that with you?"

"It's Jefferson Lockwood," Maud replied.

"Jefferson Lockwood! Jefferson Lockwood!" the man moaned the words. He dropped the gun, rushed forward and threw his arms around the still speechless boy. Jeff stiffened as the arms crushed him and his father whispered, "My son, my son."

Tears choked Jeff as he half cried, "Dad, Dad, what have you done!"

The man pulled away. He held Jeff's arms for a moment and whispered, "Hurry, you must go. Go as fast as you can. If you are followed I'll do my best to lead them away from your trail. But hurry, run!"

Still confused, Jeff took Maud's hand and moved off through the woods. The moon gave ample light for travel, and it wasn't until two hours passed that Jeff pulled up in the bottom of a rocky gully.

"Maud, that was my father," Jeff stuttered.

"I didn't know until I heard him back there, but he talked with me this afternoon."

In moody discouragement Jeff sank to the ground and buried his head in his hands, sobbing out his heartbreak, "They said he was a traitor. I didn't believe them. I didn't believe them, but now I must."

Maud kneeled beside him. "Jeff, he isn't a traitor. He talked with me and gave me a message. He isn't a traitor at all. He's on a mission for Captain Lemming. He gave me a message that must get through before the winter sets in."

Jeff raised his head only half understanding the words. He stared at Maud and asked, "What? What did you say?"

Maud explained, "This afternoon your father, only I didn't know who he was then, came to me while I pounded corn meal. He asked if I were a captive. I told him, yes. He asked if there was any possibility of my escape. I told him I had only been there a short time and had hopes of someone coming to rescue me," Maud paused.

Jeff leaned forward, his eyes intent on her, "Yes, go on."

"Well, he said he had a message that was very important and had to get to headquarters as soon as possible. He said he couldn't leave the English army yet because there was still more information needed."

The full import finally flooded Jeff's tangled thinking and with a thankful sigh he exclaimed, "Praise the Lord!"

"I'm so glad, Jeff. I'm glad you came and rescued me. It was terrible living there. The Indian women were all right, but the men were cruel. One spoke to me in his language and I couldn't understand. He hit me with a whip. A woman, who spoke English, told me what he wanted, so I escaped further beating."

Jeff interrupted, "What was the message my father gave you?"

"He said to get word to Captain Lemming to be at Fort Ticonderoga on the morning of December twenty-six. He said to use the number one-forty-two to show the authority of the message. He told me Captain Lemming would understand."

Happy relief welled in Jeff. "So, Dad made friends with that settler who favored the English just to get behind their lines and he's been gathering information all this time. Why, I knew Dad would never have betrayed his own country."

20

"He's On Our Trail!"

OVERJOYED WITH THE ASSURANCE his father was not a traitor, Jeff felt a new enthusiasm as he pushed onward in the moonlight. He chose a southeasterly direction, hoping to hit West Canada Creek. "Once on the banks of the stream it will be easy for us to work south and find the Mohawk River," Jeff told Maud. "That's where Fort Herkimer stands. We can stop there for a short rest and then swing west again to Fort Killypox."

A silvery cloud blotted out the moon, making the way harder to travel. There were many tumbles over fallen logs; bushes whipped their faces and the stitching on Maud's right moccasin broke.

When the cloud passed over the moon and the land again lay under the golden mysterious light Jeff saw a towering hill a quarter of a mile ahead.

"Maud, let's get up that hill. We can find a place to rest and from there we will be able to look back and see if we are being followed."

Maud's voice was strained with tiredness. "I'll try." The girl said nothing more as Jeff took her hand and led the way.

The steep slant of the hill was hard to ascend in the semi darkness. Twice they dropped on the ground to regain their wind. Finally they came upon a large flat rock on the hilltop.

"Maud, let me have your moccasin. I'll cut a thong of leather from my pack sack and rethread the broken seam. In the meantime, you had better get some sleep, for we'll have to push on the first thing in the morning. It would never do for one of those redskins to catch up with us. It would be our end for sure. I wish I had my musket."

"I was so afraid when that Indian saw me while I was cutting the birch bark. I started to run, but it was no use. He caught me before I had gone a hundred feet. I cried quite a bit, I guess, but then I began to pray. I've been praying ever since it seems, and I just know the Lord is with us," Maud said.

"The Lord surely answered my prayers for finding you, and also about my father. It's a heap of encouragement to a fellow to realize the Lord is always near enough to talk to, no matter how tight the spot is," Jeff added feelingly.

Jeff related his adventures from the first moment he had discovered Maud's tracks until he hid above the Indian camp, but Maud never heard the last part, for sleep had overtaken her. Jeff heard her gentle breathing and covered her with his jacket.

It was a difficult task to rethread the seam of the moccasin in the dark, but it had to be done before dawn, so Jeff kept at it until it was satisfactory. The moon had disappeared behind a grayish cloud bank and a chill wind sprang up from the north.

A crow cawed at dawn just as the work on the moccasin was done. Maud still slept, and Jeff left her on the rock while he climbed a tree to search the back trail to see if pursuers were following.

He chose a towering pine and from the tiptop he saw the Indian camp way off in the distance. Soggy smoke spirals twisted upwards telling of the arousing of the English, but even though the forest was bare of leaves, he couldn't see anyone following.

Returning, he found Maud sitting up, sleepily rubbing her eyes, "I guess I overslept," she said, shaking out her hair that had been tangled by the bushes during the flight. While she rebraided her pigtails, Jeff opened his pack and set out the remaining portions of food. They ate the cold smoked deermeat in silence.

"We are at least two days away from home and that little corn is all we have left. Perhaps we should save it until later," Jeff suggested.

Maud tucked the corn in the pocket of her jacket and Jeff hid the pack sack under tree roots. "No use carrying anything that might hold us back. Now all I have left is my knife, and I'm not sure that can do us much good."

"It looks and feels like snow," Maud commented, glancing at the leaden sky.

"I hope it doesn't. The traveling will be hard enough without snow drifts to wallow through. Besides, the moccasins we're wearing would be practically worthless," Jeff continued. "Well, Maud, we have to move along, but before we do, let's ask the Lord for help."

They kneeled and Jeff prayed aloud, asking the Lord to direct their paths and to see them through. When they arose they swung down the forested hillside.

For the most part the country was flat, only an occasional hill or gully made the traveling difficult. The sky overhead seemed to lower every minute and about noon the first flakes, big and sticky, and wet, drifted down.

Almost within minutes the soggy snow blanketed the country with a film of white. A flock of chickadees chattered nearby and a noisy jay scolded a low flying crow.

"If there's anyone on our trail we're sure to be found. Look at our tracks," Jeff said. Behind them, like a long line,

K

lay the tracks in the snow. Jeff shuddered, "And there's not a thing we can do about them."

"My feet are soaking wet, Jeff."

"Well, when we stop tonight we'll have to light a fire and dry our clothes."

As the afternoon wore on, the country became more rolling. At the top of one of the hills Jeff looked back. "Maud, look!" he exclaimed. "Look, back there. See that Indian? He's on our trail!"

Maud, trembling with concern asked, "What can we do?"

"I don't know. Look, he's running. He doesn't see us yet." Indeed, the Indian was flying over the trail. There was no doubt about his being able to catch up to them.

Jeff dragged Maud after him, running down a steep slope. "We have to get to some place and hide."

A huge boulder appeared off to the left. Jeff bypassed it and then circled back and squatted behind the protection. He shoved Maud underneath a jutting corner of the stone. Then he peeked over the top. The Indian bounded over the rise and came into full view. He carried a bow, but no musket. His clothes were of buckskin. He wore a belt around the jacket. Jeff saw a tomahawk and a knife dangling from it.

The warrior swept close, so close Jeff could see the scalp lock and the long hooked nose and the high bronze cheek bones. Suddenly Jeff crouched down. The padding footsteps drifted to him. He waited. There was only one thing to do. Surprise the redskin and take the offensive.

Fifty feet, forty, thirty, twenty, ten, *Now!* Jeff leaped out and smashed into the enemy. The redskin shrieked defiance and twisted violently to escape Jeff's hands. Jeff caught the Indian's right arm and drew it back, but had to release the grip when the Indian managed to free the tomahawk. The stone weapon crashed toward Jeff's head, missing by a fraction of an inch.

The tomahawk raised again, but Jeff swung his right fist at the pointed nose. The blow staggered the Indian and Jeff leaped upon him, wresting the weapon from his hand and flinging it away.

Now the redskin felt for the knife. Again and again Jeff pounded his face; the knife flashed up and Jeff grabbed the long thin fingers that held it and forced them backwards over the wrist. The knife fell in the snow. Jeff lunged in again as the Indian stooped to regain the weapon. The knife slithered off to one side. The Indian dropped to the ground and crawled amid raining blows to the spot. Jeff kicked the knife out of reach. Suddenly the Mohawk rolled on his back, doubled his legs and kicked. The blow caught Jeff in the pit of the stomach, sending him reeling and groggy back over a fallen tree.

With a shriek the warrior pounced forward, his long fingers finding Jeff's throat. The fingers tightened. Blindly Jeff swung upward at the face.

Jeff's breath left him, his eyes seemed to bulge from their sockets and a strange fainting feeling engulfed him.

A sudden dull thud sounded, the fingers released and the Indian rolled to one side. Jeff sucked in lungs full of air. He opened his eyes and saw Maud's tear-stained face above. She held a heavy piece of wood in her hand.

Jeff struggled to his feet and pinned the savages arms behind him and tied them fast with the redskin's belt. Jeff gasped, "You sure hit him. Why, you saved my life." His words carried his admiration of Maud's courage.

"What can we do to him?" Maud asked.

"Most people would kill him, but I couldn't," Jeff said, rubbing his stiffened neck. "I guess the only thing we can do is leave him here. The Indians back at the camp will come out and find him."

Jeff found the tomahawk and knife and threw them as

far away as he could. "We'll take his bow and arrow along with us just in case." Jeff said.

"He'll freeze lying on the ground like that." Maud said.

"Well, I'll cut some pine boughs and fix a place for him." As Jeff spoke the Indian opened his eyes and stared blankly at his conquerors. There seemed to be a look of respect in them, but a look of respect mixed with fear.

Jeff asked, "Do you speak English?"

A grunting mumble was the only reply.

Jeff recognized the Indian's term for yes, so he continued, "Other men would kill you and leave you to the foxes and crows, but I am a follower of the Lord Jesus Christ, so I cannot. We are going to leave you here, bound so you cannot move, so your people can find you."

Jeff hurriedly cut an armful of pine boughs and made a leanto. They lined it with more boughs and dragged the Indian into it. When they walked away the snow was two inches deep and as they traveled the snow covered up the trail almost as soon as it was made.

Evening found them by a narrow stream, not yet frozen over. Jeff exclaimed, "This must be West Canada Creek. We'll camp here for the night."

"Do you think it's safe to light a fire?" Maud inquired, twisting the tails of her jacket until the melted snow water dripped down in stained riverlets.

"We'll have to get dry. We'd both perish if we slept in these clothes." Jeff drew his knife and began to prepare wood peelings for the fire. The snow continued to sift downward. The trees were mantled in layers of white, dulling sound to such an extent that their breathing was almost loud in the silence. The few handfuls of corn were all they had to eat, but with their clothes dry they didn't feel so bad, and they bowed their heads to thank the Lord for what they had.

"Maud, if I'm not mistaken we have about fifteen miles

to go directly south. We should be able to cover that distance tomorrow if the snow doesn't get too deep."

The fire glowed against the west bank of the stream and Jeff walked a few hundred yards away to see if it could be seen. When he returned he said, "I doubt if the fire can be spotted. But I'll stand guard and scout around a bit."

The following morning they pushed along the stream for a mile. Jeff had been up the whole night. When the snow stopped, and the sun peered through the clouds, he halted.

"Something's wrong," he muttered. "West Canada Creek runs generally straight south, but this stream is veering west."

"Are you sure?" Maud questioned.

"Positive. We're on the wrong brook." Jeff's face wrinkled in doubt. "I'm afraid we're lost."

He glanced at the sun. According to his figuring they were headed directly away from Killypox. He swung about taking a southerly route. Now the sun was off to his left. All day they traveled, pushing through the snow for miles and miles of endless forest. Along the way they saw a couple of squirrels and Jeff tried to shoot them with the bow he had taken from the Indian, but each time the arrows fell short.

"We'll have to find something to eat soon or we'll be too exhausted and hungry to travel. I think we had better build a fire and I'll try to stalk something to get close enough for a shot."

After the fire was started he left Maud drying her feet while he struck off in the woods. The air was biting cold and the snow crunched under his sodden moccasins. He found a place in an oak grove where squirrels were plentiful and squatted near a tree, with an arrow ready on the bow.

A blue jay, his brilliant blue and white feathers standing out sharply against the snow, hopped to a limb six feet above his head. The bow was drawn taut and an arrow flew, catching the bird broadsides and dropping it to the snow. Jeff picked it up and returned to wait for a squirrel.

One big fluffy gray squirrel scampered down a tree and raced through the snow toward another about twenty feet in front of Jeff. He raised the bow and the string twanged in the sharp air. The arrow buried itself in a sapling off to the right. The squirrel chattered a warning and flicked up a tree and out of sight. An hour passed and the cold bit into Jeff. He shivered, teeth chattering, and his feet grew numb. Discouraged with his success he plodded back to the fire.

"All I got was this blue jay. He sure doesn't look like a meal."

"I'll help," Maud said, taking the bird and plucking the feathers. With a stick through the middle of the tiny carcass Maud turned it over the flame until it was an even brown. After thanking the Lord they divided the bird in half, eating it in silence, even chewing the bones for the last bit of nourishment.

21

"I'll Be Back"

AFTER THE LAST of the blue jay disappeared, they pushed southward. The afternoon sun shimmered on the white snow. They waded through the drifts until evening closed in. A fire cheered them but little. Jeff propped their moccasins on sticks and turned them continually so they would not burn.

"I'm sorry I didn't hold on to my musket. At least I could hit a few of the squirrels we have seen," Jeff said.

"I wonder how far we have to go to get home." Maud coughed as she spoke.

"I don't know, but if we go south far enough we're bound to hit the Mohawk River sometime."

When the moccasins dried out they smothered the fire with snow and trudged through the barren forest, silent and worried. Jeff knew Maud was catching cold. He knew also the pinched feeling he had in his stomach was hunger, and although Maud hadn't complained he felt sure she was suffering more than he.

A whir-r-r-r of beating wings flared a few feet ahead of him. Jeff tensed as he saw a spruce grouse fly to a low-hanging limb. He strung an arrow and with Maud standing motionless, he edged forward, praying as he went. The bird, a rufus red color, gazed blankly at him. At fifteen feet he stopped and took careful aim. The arrow sang straight and true, plunging into the bird.

Jeff leaped forward and caught the struggling bird.
With a cry of happiness Maud almost shouted, "Food!"

At her words, another grouse hurtled from a snow
bank and plunged into a pine tree. Again Jeff crept forward,
bow ready. He saw the bird squatting on a dark green bough.
He let the arrow fly. The bird didn't move a feather as the
arrow whined over its head. He readied another arrow and
edged forth. Breathless with desire, and trembling with hope,
Jeff again asked the Lord for help. The arrow left the
bow, darting into the bird's plump breast.

As Maud plucked and cleaned the birds, Jeff built the
fire and said, "I'm sure glad that spruce grouse have no fear
of man like other birds. If they did, we'd never have this
feast."

When the birds were ready, the two young people
poured out hearts filled with thanksgiving before they ate.

After the meal was completed they pushed on again
but within minutes Maud stopped and said, "I smell smoke
and something cooking."

"It isn't from our fire, that's for sure, and the wind is
blowing from the southwest, so that means the smell's coming
from that direction. Let's head that way and see."

They struggled against the drifts, working their way up
and down a shallow gully, running north and south.

It was Jeff who shouted, "Say, I know where we are.
This is where I shot the deer and bear. Home is two miles
south of here!"

Fired with this knowledge, they plunged through a
pine grove. Ahead a trail of smoke lifted to the sky. Jeff
shouted, "Hello, Mr. Watson!" An echo drifted back to them,
"Hello, Mr. Watson!"

Then far off, a voice carried back, "Hello-o-o-o-o!"

"Praise the Lord, it's Dad!" Maud shouted.

Within minutes, Mr. Watson and Carl Ives crashed
through the underbrush. Jeff saw tears running freely down

Maud's cheeks and he felt salty drops of his own, as he gripped the hands of Carl and the missionary.

"We were just about getting underway to search for you," Carl explained on their way home.

"Are Mother and Pam at the fort?" Maud asked.

"Yes, we left them there, but we planned to return home as soon as you were found. That place is so crowded down there it's the best thing to do," Mr. Watson answered.

Back home around a roaring fire, and between mouthfuls of food, Maud and Jeff took turns telling of their experiences. Carl and Mr. Watson thrilled at the account, and both commended Jeff for his work.

When the story was complete, Carl said, "Jeff, the Killypox militia captured a number of the enemy. Among them was the fat-faced Kittle. They're taking him to prison in Albany."

"So, all his plans for the future are ruined. It sure proves that following an evil plan leads to a bitter end," Jeff said.

With a radiant feeling of joy they traveled to Fort Killypox where Mrs. Watson cried for happiness.

Captain Snow begrudgingly admitted Jeff had done a wonderful job. "In spite of the fact your father is a traitor, I guess you're all right," he bellowed.

Jeff smiled, knowing that when spring came and all the truth was known, his father would be acclaimed a hero by the very ones who now spoke against him.

He told Carl of the message. "I have to leave right away to get it to Captain Lemming."

"It will be rough traveling with snow on the ground, but you can make it," Carl laughed. "After all, with your Dad succeeding in tricking the English, I reckon there's nothing a Lockwood can't do."

For two days Jeff rested, and then on the third morning he helped the Watsons back to their home. Carl promised to help Mr. Watson put up the new cabin.

They arrived at noon and sat around the fire eating dinner, when Jeff glanced toward the brook. He saw three figures outlined dark against the snow. A wave of dread gripped him, for they were Mohawks, clad in blankets.

Mrs. Watson gasped, covering Pam with a blanket. Carl rose to his feet. One of the Indian warriors stepped forward and held his hand above his head. Then Jeff recognized Wigo, the same brave whose life he had saved. Now he had come back to attack.

They watched Wigo step thirty feet forward from the other two. With slow deliberate motions Wigo took a handful of arrows from his quiver and raised them in the air. He snapped them and cast the broken ends to the snow.

Jeff sprang forward. "It's a sign of peace!"

Wigo and the two braves walked forward solemnly. They came directly before Mr. Watson and Wigo spoke in English. "I escape those who took me east. I return to my village. I think. I think much. I remember what you tell me of Jesus Christ. I know you speak truth. I accepted Jesus as my Lord. Now I bring two of my tribal brothers so they can hear also."

The Indians stayed the greater part of the day and listened as Mr. Watson told them of the Saviour, Jesus Christ. Before they faded into the forest, all professed to acknowledge the Lord as Master of their lives.

The next morning the sun glinted silver white on the snow. Jeff's pack was in readiness as he pulled a warm beaver skin hat down over his ears.

Mrs. Watson kissed him lightly, "Jeff, we'll be remembering you every day in our prayers."

Carl grasped his hand, "Come back as early as you can in the spring."

Mr Lockwood pulled on his boots as he said, "Well, after a good meal we'll be off, Captain Snow."

"Good, and the next time you come west be sure and stop by Killypox. You'll both be welcome."

Within an hour Jeff and his Dad were swinging east on the horses generously supplied by Captain Snow.

Sam Lockwood spoke softly as they moved along the frozen Mohawk River. "The Lord has been good to me, Jeff. He's enabled me to help in our resistance against slavery."

"He's been good to me also, Dad. I have learned a lot in the last seven months and I'm coming out again as soon as I can and help Mr. Watson do missionary work among the settlers and Indians."

His father smiled contentedly. "Splendid, for I plan to bring Mother and Mary out next spring."

"Everything's worked out perfectly," Jeff said aloud. Then to himself he thanked the Lord for returning his father to him — not a traitor, but rather a real hero. Yes, the Lord certainly was good.

Jeff was so startled by this unexpected welcome that he stood motionless for a moment. Then he saw Lumberkin rushing from the blockhouse and the scout's weather beaten face relaxed in a broad grin. "Jeff Lockwood, I'm apologizing to you for my ways last summer."

Jeff sputtered in confusion, "Why? What?"

"Surprised by all this, young feller?" Captain Snow bellowed.

"Yes," Jeff admitted.

"We know a lot more than we did. Come, boy, I'll show ya' something."

Jeff followed as the Captain and the scout headed for one of the log buildings. Captain Snow laid a finger across his lips, indicating his desire for silence and then stepped inside. At first Jeff could see nothing, for there was little light. Then as his eyes adjusted themselves, he saw a bed with someone in it, off to one side.

Suddenly an explosive exclamation came from his lips.

"Dad! Dad!" he cried as he sprang forward and threw his arms around the sleeping man.

His father awoke, "Jeff, you made it back safely?"

"Yes," was all that Jeff could say.

"And how about the girl?" his father questioned.

"Maud's fine, Dad, but how did you get here?"

"Well, shortly after you escaped, I found out the plan the English have for a spring attack. With this information, my work was done. I feel certain our army will be able to successfully defeat them next year. So I slipped away shortly after you did and now I must get to Captain Lemming as soon as possible with this material, and then we'll head for home."

"Won't Mother and Mary be glad to see us walk in!" Jeff sighed.

"And won't I be glad to see them?"

"I will too," Jeff agreed.

"Do that, Jeff, and plan to stay with us," Mr. Watson agreed.

"I'll be back. Nothing could keep me away but it won't be for the same reasons I had when I came out here last spring. I'm coming back to build a home in this wonderful wilderness land, but I have a greater reason than that. After seeing Wigo and his red brothers change from enemies to friends because they accepted the Lord Jesus Christ, I want to come back and help you do missionary work among them."

"Good, I'll need help," Mr. Watson said.

Jeff kissed Pam and turned toward the east. Maud walked with him, until they reached the edge of the clearing. Tears filled Maud's eyes and her voice was husky, "Jeff, I'll be looking for you when the first maple leaf unfurls next spring."

"I'll be back, Maud."

He waved to the folks, and broke into a trot eastward through the snow.

The brilliant sun glistened on the white snow, a fiery red cardinal whistled from a leafless maple. These things were pleasant, but Jeff's heart throbbed with joy for deeper reasons.

Dad is a hero instead of a traitor. Won't Mother and Mary be glad when I walk in with that news! Then next spring I'll be coming back here to this wonderful country, Jeff thought as he moved along the edge of a ravine.

His first impulse was to skirt Fort Killypox and avoid the antagonism of Lumberkin and Captain Snow. Yet, this would take him out of his way and he was anxious to get to Captain Lemming as soon as possible.

By noon he stood at the log gate. The sentry had seen him and within moments the door swung open.

Captain Snow stood there and, to Jeff's amazement, extended a huge paw-like hand. He exclaimed, "Jeff, my boy, good it is that you're here again. Come in! Come in!"